Gardens from the Sand

Gardens from the Sand

A Story About Looking
for Answers & Finding Miracles

∾

DAN CAVICCHIO

HarperSanFrancisco
A Division of HarperCollins*Publishers*

The epigraph is quoted from *A Course in Miracles* (Glen Ellen, CA: Foundation for Inner Peace, 1975).

GARDENS FROM THE SAND: *A Story About Looking for Answers & Finding Miracles.* Copyright © 1994 by Dan Cavicchio. All rights reserved. Printed in the United States of America. No part of this book may be used or reproduced in any manner whatsoever without written permission except in the case of brief quotations embodied in critical articles and reviews. For information address HarperCollins Publishers, 10 East 53rd Street, New York, NY 10022.

Book design by Eric Holub

FIRST EDITION

Library of Congress Cataloging-in-Publication Data

Cavicchio, Dan.

Gardens from the sand : a story about looking for answers & finding miracles / Dan Cavicchio.

p. cm.

ISBN 0–06–251053–3 (pbk. : alk. paper)

I. Title.

PS3553.A967637 1994

813'.54—dc20   94–9288

94 95 96 97 98 ❖ RRD(H) 10 9 8 7 6 5 4 3 2 1

This edition is printed on acid-free paper that meets the American National Standards Institute Z39.48 Standard.

I wish to extend my deepest gratitude to
Mallika, Gautam, Rita and Deepak Chopra;
to Lynn, John and Karen;
and to my friends and family, new and old.
Thank you for your loving support.

"See how life springs up everywhere!
The desert becomes a garden,
green and deep and quiet,
offering rest to those
who lost their way
and wander in
the dust."

∽

A Course in Miracles

Gardens from the Sand

ONE

A man once took the final step of a thousand-mile journey atop a lonely desert knoll. First he fell to his knees; then, whispering some lost words to the wind, he bent low and touched his lips to the ground. From a sack at his waist he took out a small seed.

The man studied the seed for a while, twirling the little thing between his thumb and first finger. He considered a world of possibilities. He dreamed of the days to come. At last, expelling a breath, he drove the seed deep into its anointed spot and covered the place with two handfuls of sand.

As the man stood and smiled, blowing the silvery grains from his hands, the evening passed quietly into the shadows of dusk.

∾

In time he built a house near the spot where the seed was planted. Sun-baked walls, a small foundation, open-air windows: the structure was modest, but it provided a cool escape for its builder. When the man finished raising his shelter, he turned diligently to the earth.

Rifts were cut in the dry ground. Holding basins were dug and banked. Silt dams were constructed out of loose rocks and debris. Each day the silhouette on the hill worked and waited and watched time blow by. When at last the rains broke, he dropped his head in gratitude.

The desert area surrounding his house was sparsely populated, but such an unexpected event as rain caused a spurt of activity. "What do you make of this?" the people asked each other, scurrying over the hills with upraised palms and nervously shaking heads. All in all, three weeks of showers hit the sand that spring. Only a handful of the oldest grandparents had seen it before; none but the children anticipated its return.

Happily, the children's faith prevailed. The rains came doubly hard the next year with a series of sprinkles every few weeks between. By the time the local almanacs had been updated, a community of seedlings had sprouted next to the man-of-the-hill's house and along the edges of his ditches. It was almost a year from the day he arrived that he finally received a visitor.

"Are you trying to grow something?" she asked from behind him. He turned and recognized the daughter of a distant neighbor.

The man took a deep smiling breath and began. "Yes. I'm going to grow a garden here on this hill. Please come and visit whenever you want." Then he paused, looking thoughtful. "I know that people may think it's crazy, this being a hillside in a desert and all. But I think it will work." His creased brow relaxed. "Yes, you know, I'm pretty certain it'll work."

"Great," she said. "Need some help?" That was all that passed between the two over the course of the afternoon. The man gathered strength from his quiet little helper. After a few hours she stood and informed him that she was going to leave, and that she'd come and visit again. He was glad.

She brought a friend with her on the next visit, and a different one on the next, and before long he was receiving a steady stream of helping hands. In time, every child within walking distance had visited the man's hillside plot. The fragrant Desert Prince's Plume was the first to blossom, and the caretaker gave its wispy yellow flowers to the delighted children. Other buds opened to receive a warm welcome. A day came when the man smiled and shook his head slowly—for it was true. Rising green upon the golden earth, the little garden had begun.

Several years later, by the time the man's creation covered the hill and spilled far into the smooth desert plain, the adults were arriving in buzzing droves. "The legends spoke of this!" they chattered excitedly to each other. "We *knew* that life would return to this sand!"

Tales were spun and spread, and visitors came from distant places to spend time with the man who tended his remarkable desert garden and spoke as he worked of green kingdoms to come. The man's words were reassuring, and the faith that flowed through them carried an empowering spirit of tenderness and hope. For this the people came. For this they traveled miles, unlaced the weary ties that bound their spirits, and flew to the skies with the desert gardener.

This man who drew life from a dry and dusty earth was one who found his way. This is the story of his discovery.

∾

On the day of his birth, the land rejoiced.

A bright morning sun beamed down on fields of dancing grass. The few clouds that dared appear were purely white puffs in a fantastically blue sky. Members of the community lined up early, hoping to be among the first to pay their respects. The land grew quiet as everyone waited.

At long last the word came: "It's here! A boy! It's a beautiful boy!" A procession began its march at once and proceeded to sweep every willing participant into its wake. The people loved holidays, and surely, they decided, an event such as this merited a day's vacation.

The birth itself took place in an open-air pavilion of the great house. The young woman had stared at the sky all night, making wishes on the stars. "I want him to be strong," she had thought, remembering the belly-kicks of recent days. "I want him to be wise . . . honest . . . generous . . . trusting . . . " So it went, throughout the night. Sometime after the break of day, she heaved one last push and decided, "I want him to be aware, like his father." With that, the child was born.

He set his lungs to work at once, inhaling the scents of morning and shooting them back into the world with a scream. Lights quickly dotted on in the house. The infant's father, having quite helplessly fallen asleep, rose from the shadows and rushed to his wife's side.

He stared at the woman and child until an old nursemaid nudged him. "Go ahead," she whispered. The man paused for a moment. Then, holding his hands out, he reached for his son. "So small," he said. He smiled at his wife. "He's so small."

And so the day went, rich with joy and tender tears. The infant slept for hours in the ancient family cradle while a line of adults shuffled by. Some offered congratulatory words to the parents; others simply nodded with warm understanding. All were enchanted by the tiny gift. Toward the end of the day, as the line was dissolving into wayward pairs and threes, one of the local seers approached and offered a handful of seeds. "For the mother and child," she explained. "They will produce many fruits."

As she ambled away, the father recalled his own birth prophecy. *Rule the lands or rise above,* his parents had been told by this same seer. *The choice is his.* The man still wondered at the words, but somehow trusted their source.

As for the child, whose eyes were blue and bright as the sky—his radiant mother named him Clare.

"Clare?" asked his father.

"Yes, Clare," said his mother. She turned to look at her child. "Look at his eyes—they're so clear. He'll see things that others miss."

The father considered her words. He was a man of prudence, and was not one to make a decision lightly. He looked at his son. For a moment the child's eyes opened, and the man saw, and he knew that his wife was right. "Clare," he whispered to himself.

"He'll brighten the world," said the woman. "I just know it."

The man continued to look at the child, and slowly, unexpectedly, his face clouded. "Yes," he said after a minute. "Yes, I hope he will."

Now the woman turned to look at her husband. The man was graced with so many gifts; he was so respected and loved. But something troubled him, something deep and hidden. Only at rare times like this did she glimpse it.

She reached for his hand. "Don't worry."

The man touched his child's head. "The world can be a difficult place. It can be so cruel."

"He'll be fine," said the woman.

The man nodded. "Yes, you're right." Then he added, "I just wish I could make it easier for him."

"You will," she said. "Somehow you will."

∾

Life flowed throughout the child's world. His mother was right, of course: Clare was quite a gifted boy.

At an early age he began to explore. There were tall forests, running streams, and wide fields to investigate. There were grasshoppers to bounce after and chattering birds to observe. The trees called him to climb them; the flowers beckoned him with their scents. The child openly embraced it all.

He ranged over the hills like some happy little shepherd. He lay on his back, gazing deeply into the sky. He dug through the dirt, looked for fish in the stream, and ran circles and circles around the pond. Never was there a dull moment in his life.

The child's world was alive, colorful, and filled with wonders—perhaps the greatest of which was the garden. Clare had helped his mother plant the first few seeds; now the garden was a world of its own.

There were a thousand diversions within the little plot of land. Aphids negotiated with ants on the stems of the golden sunflowers. Sticky larvae pulsed and glistened on leaves lit by the morning sun. Fat worms dug through the soil, popping occasionally to the surface for a visit.

The boy had a game that he loved to play in the garden: first he'd find an interesting stick and draw a circle around himself in the dirt. Then he'd sit within the circle for hours, greeting every leaf and bug that happened to fall into his realm.

"Hello, bug," he said one day to a spotted beetle. "What have you seen today?"

The boy had a long-running argument with his schoolteacher about bugs. The man said bugs couldn't talk. However, Clare knew he was wrong. When he spoke to a bug, the bug spoke back. The voice wasn't loud or soft, like the things he heard with his ears, but it certainly sounded as clear.

Today the bug said something like this: "I've been flying around all morning. I've seen some baby sparrows in a treetop nest, and some bees in a crack in the wall. I wish you could come see them with me."

"I can't," said the child wistfully. "But tell me what it looks like inside of a beehive and a nest. I want to know."

So the bug stayed and spoke with Clare until it finally wandered outside of the circle. Then the boy could hear it no more. "Hello, rock," he said to a half-buried stone. The rocks stayed and talked forever, but they really didn't have much to say—they hadn't been around. "Hello, fly," he said, and so it went for the rest of the afternoon.

Though few people understood it at the time, Clare was born into an exceptional breed of children: he was an explorer. His life was a constant discovery and his vision captured all.

Each sunrise that passed before the youngster's sleepy eyes entranced him with its originality. A long-legged spider could engage him for hours. He took nothing for granted, and not one thing in his life ever entered the realm of the mundane.

When he wasn't chasing birds, the child spent his afternoons sprawled among the dandelions. He oversaw the summer's growing grass and the winter's long snowmelt. Nothing escaped the young master's attention.

He listened and heard music in the babbling stream. He tasted and found the essence of the fruit. He ran his hands over smooth stone walls and prickly thistles with the same trusting abandon. Although he never told anyone, he liked to smell horse dung as much as the roses.

There was just so much to be uncovered and appreciated: crystal frost, tiny brown tadpoles; even the races of the clouds across the sky provided delight for the little one who chose to see.

∽

"What *do* you see?" asked his mother one day. The boy had been standing in front of an oak tree for almost half an hour.

He whispered to her, "There. In the vines."

The woman glanced at the ivy-strewn tree. It was quite ordinary; she had passed it hundreds of times on the way to town.

But now, intrigued, she looked more closely. She scanned the leaves of ivy, deep and shiny in the late-August sun. A family of tendrils had sprouted off from the vine to wrap around the tree; some were curled into corkscrews, and the rest were searching straight and wide for a mate. It *was* a pretty patch of ivy—this she had to admit. And the tree, so close, looked wise and old. She smiled upon the ancient oak and was suddenly glad for its presence.

"There," Clare whispered again. "There, in the ivy."

She traced his vision to a point, but could see nothing. Then a tiny gray bubble moved. She lowered her head, searched, and finally found a half-opened cocoon among the leaves.

"He's coming out, isn't he?" she asked.

Clare nodded. "I've been watching every day for a week."

The woman smiled and rustled his hair. "Keep a good eye on him; you may learn something important. I'll be in the garden."

"OK," he said softly without moving his eyes. And the woman walked off toward the vegetables.

∼

Clare's mother began her garden on the day her husband left. It had been a great source of comfort for her—the first four rows of carrots had helped immeasurably to ease her fears.

She hadn't been surprised to wake to an empty bed that day, for somehow she knew her husband was going to leave. And she knew that someday he'd be back. But on the day he left, she had been almost overwhelmed with concern—for him and his journey, and especially for her son. The carrots had helped.

In time she dismissed the family servants and closed off most of the old house—to her, the old lifestyle felt unnecessarily grand. As the days passed, she found herself turning more frequently to her garden. The garden was a place of stillness, a place of rest. It was a place where she could be with her child, and—when he wasn't around—with the vegetables. It was a safe section of the world, a place where she could build and grow.

The garden was also a place of healing; for, though she accepted the flow of life around her, she wasn't without a feeling of loss. Her husband was gone, passed into time like the summer. She fully met the new season, but she also paused at times, and escaped into the garden, and allowed herself the room to heal.

The woman planted carrots first, and by the time their lacy green tops reached the height of her shins they shared the space with a young cohort of beets. Next came green bunches of lettuce ringed by shining orange marigolds. Red-leafed lettuce followed, then several tight balls of cabbage. It gave her strength to watch it unfold.

When Clare was six, he helped her build a white wooden trellis for vines of snow peas to climb. They kept pace with the height of the growing boy until early fall; then they bowed before him and retreated back into the earth. Swiss chard was one of the garden's most unusual inhabitants until the herb garden evolved. Richly diverse, it brought together the roots of the world's spices.

The little herb garden provided a place for another of the child's games. It was simple: closing his eyes, Clare would bend over a particular plant and carefully draw two or three deep breaths through his nose. The smells freed his imagination to soar.

The scent of basil, for example, conjured royal, exotic images in his mind. It was an alluring and somewhat disturbing smell, very different from the sweet aroma of lemon balm. Blue sage and tall yellow mustard plants beckoned him with colored explosions, spilling forth the spirits of hot, dusty places. Peppermint, of course, was a favorite, along with its licorice-flavored cousin anise. Thyme, tarragon, caraway, dill—all enriched his beloved world.

Clare and his mother spent much of their time in the garden, sharing ideas as they worked. The boy hungered for knowledge; luckily, his mother was a woman of wisdom who rarely missed an opportunity to turn a question into a lesson. The child learned quickly under her watchful eye.

"Isn't he pretty, Clare?" she asked late one afternoon, cupping a ghostly white spider in her hands.

"Yes," said Clare, licking his fingers. "Mom," he then announced, "you know, I really don't like school very much." She was pulling weeds and he was cleaning a clay mixing bowl of its chocolate mess. He must have been seven years old.

"Is that true?" she replied, returning the spider to its onion patch.

"Yeah. You know," he shrugged, "it's not very fun. We don't learn about anything important. I'd rather be outside looking at the things I like."

"Like the bugs?"

"Yeah, like the bugs and the pebbles in the stream. And that butterfly I found in the tree. And the hawks. There's just so much to see outside. And there's barely anything to see inside." He tossed the bowl onto the grass. "I just get so *bored*."

She considered his words. Then she said, "The problem could be your attitude." He gave her a puzzled look, so she went on. "When you're sitting at your desk in school, you probably don't feel in charge of things, do you?"

"Well, no, not really." He began clutching handfuls of dirt, looking for worms.

"You have to ask for permission to go to the bathroom. And you have to raise your hand if you want to speak, right?"

"Well, yeah. I guess."

She smiled at him. "Giving someone control over your life like that is bound to create frustration."

"But mom," he protested, standing up. "I'm not *giving* Mr. Tugtime control over me. He just *has* it."

"Do you really think so?"

"Of course!" he said. "I have to go to school, and I can't just get up and leave if I want."

"Clare," she said, "you really don't *have* to do anything."

A moment of confusion passed into joy. Not go to school! Now that was a brilliant idea. He took it from several angles, then narrowed his eyes and presented her with the following:

"So wait. Are you saying I don't have to go to school tomorrow if I don't want to?"

"Yes."

"What?" he cried, jumping up. "Why didn't you ever tell me this before?"

"Clare," she laughed, "I've never made you do anything; you just assumed that it was the only way. Now you're learning." She smiled at the expression on his face.

This was a weighty concept, so he sat down and pondered it for a while. He figured that there must be a loophole somewhere. Otherwise, he had wasted too much of his little life sitting in a classroom.

"Anyway," she went on, "when someone is feeling

frustrated they usually say 'I'm bored.' As if some little gray cloud had come to sit on their shoulders. It's like Kat—I think she spends a lot of her time being bored, especially when she can't catch those mice. Have you ever seen her sitting in the corner, yawning to death?" The woman chuckled at the image. "You'd think that our mice weren't enough of a challenge."

Clare was still thinking about missing school, running scenarios through his mind. He could wander down to the pond tomorrow and skip stones, or climb the forked maple, or . . . At that point, a scary idea hit him.

"Mom, what if Mr. Tugtime gets mad at me?"

"I suppose that *is* a risk involved," she admitted. She thought for a minute. "Here," she said, "why don't you do this: whenever you hear the call, just raise your hand and ask to go to the bathroom. Then go outside and wander around until you're content. I'll write a note to Mr. Tugtime telling him that you're having some digestive problems. Which you might," she added, looking at the empty mixing bowl.

He brightened. "Great! Thanks."

"Sure. Now, do you want to come help me pull some weeds?"

A sly look flickered across his face, and was quickly gone. "No," he said. "I don't."

She grinned and nodded, returning to her work. "Fine."

"I'm just kidding!" he cried. He ran up and put his arms around her in a bearlike embrace. Her ribs were glad that the child was still small. Together, happily, they worked for the rest of the afternoon.

∾

Clare's mother routinely picked and dried herbs on Monday, harvested the mature vegetables each Friday, and sold the goods at a local market on the weekend. She had little need for the money it brought; however, she thoroughly enjoyed sharing her garden's gifts. Her produce was given high marks by the community and rarely did she return home with unsold stocks.

The boy grew to love the market, for it was almost as rich in sights and sounds as the garden. Loud men with bronze complexions and strange accents bantered back and forth, swearing on the quality of their goods. Artists proudly displayed their sculptures and paintings; usually they didn't mind if people handled their work. The air smelled of sweat and spicy food. It was a bustling, energetic place, full of shadowy alleys to explore and interesting people to watch. The garden at home was wonderfully tranquil, but the excitement of the market square played an important counterpoint in his life.

The boy prided himself on finding the most unorthodox path between two points. He climbed over wooden wagons and crawled through dry drainage ditches. He hid in shadows, straining to remain motionless and unnoticed by the sidewalk parade. Hopping with one foot on carefully selected cobblestones, the little explorer traced his way through the neglected corners of the village.

By evening, his pockets were unfailingly full of discoveries—a small blue star found on a doorstep, broken shards of amber glass, three cat's-eye marbles rescued from the gutter. Returning home, he stored his sacred treasures in a box under his bed.

One day, late in Clare's childhood, his mother sent him into town alone to buy seeds. Arriving in the village after a substantial hike, the boy marched straight across Main Street to the familiar sign lettered SPICES, SEEDS, ETCETERA.

A chime sounded as he walked in.

"Hello, Mr. Tannen!"

"Eh? Clare! Hello!" the man offered with squinting eyes. "Here all alone today?"

"Yep." His pride showed.

"How's school these days?"

"Oh, it's fine." The boy averaged two to three daily walkabouts, and succeeded in keeping his spirit sufficiently content. His schoolteacher had long since discovered the true nature of Clare's bathroom visits, but wisely allowed the pretense to go unchallenged.

"That's good. What can I get for you today?"

Reading from a list, the boy rattled off a variety of seeds. The old proprietor raced around his store, pulling dusty jars from nooks and high shelves. Finally finished, out of breath, he frowned, "Your mother sure asks for the best. I don't know anyone else around here who uses most of these." Placing the seeds in small bags, he wrapped the purchases together in a sheet of brown paper. "Here you are, young man," he called, sliding the package across his counter.

Clare was on the other side of the store, inhaling the air of a coffee-bean jar. "Where does this come from?" he asked. "It makes me think of a jungle."

The owner raised the countertop and shuffled over to the container. "That one's from an island in the Pacific Ocean called Hawaii. Special order, you know."

15

Clare smelled another. "And this?"

"From Colombia, a country in the south. That one is too. And this one's from Africa."

"Tigers and elephants Africa?"

"Ha. Yes, I suppose so," replied the man. "Although I saw neither when I was there."

"You were *there?* In *Africa?*" It was hard for him to imagine old Mr. Tannen cavorting about in the land of tigers and elephants.

"Sure. I've been around the world and back, Clare. That's how I made connections to import my merchandise."

"Did you go exploring, though?" he demanded eagerly. "Did you see new trees and bugs? Were there mountains to climb? Did you sail across the ocean?"

The face of old Mr. Tannen spread into a smile. Something in the child's voice drew forth his aged memories, still overflowing with boundless hopes and dreams. He took a seat upon a stool and, for ten minutes, told an inspired tale of pirates and stowaways, of dark caves and temples, of peaks and valleys and wide, wide oceans. Some of it had happened; the rest was drawn from stories told to him as a boy. It was a bold, rollicking adventure, and it effectively swept the awestruck listener into another life. Like the young Tannen child so many years before, Clare was now indelibly marked by the mystique of Abroad.

◌◌

The conversations in the garden soon became overwhelmed by Clare's inquiries. "Where does this come from, mom?" he asked as he flipped through the empty seed packets. "What's it like over there? What about this one?"

His mother, had she been a walking travelogue, couldn't have answered the barrage of questions that assaulted her. She had expected her son to outgrow the little plot of land; however, she had hoped that the time wouldn't come so quickly. She decided that it was time to explain.

"Clare, please sit down," she said, patting the seat of a wooden chair. "We need to have a talk." This was not long after the boy's visit to the seed shop, and his eyes still shone with awe. "You were so young back then," she said, "but you must remember your father."

Clare's mind raced as his eyes struck the ground. This was certainly unexpected. Yes, he did remember: the servants, his father's regal presence; the love that everyone showered on the man, the trust that each one placed at his feet. And he remembered the loss, the terrible sadness which began with five of the chief horseman's words. "The master has left us," the horseman had announced in confusion. "Forever." Over and over the burly man repeated it. "He has left us." It was one of the oldest images in Clare's mind, and also one of the clearest. He could still see the figure, dressed in his father's tight-fitting clothes, beginning to tremble with tears.

"Yes," said the boy tersely. "I remember him leaving."

"Do you know why he left?"

"No." Many years ago he had given up wondering. "Why—do you?"

"I think I do," she replied with weighed conviction. Her husband's boyish face returned through the years, and she studied it as she spoke. "There had been something in your father's eyes for a long time—a question,

I guess." She searched for the right words. "Your father had a lot of questions."

Clare ran a thumbnail across his teeth. He frowned, waiting for her to go on.

"He thought a lot about the world," the woman continued. "He used to ask me things like, 'Why does everyone struggle so much?' and 'What can we do to help?' Your father asked so many questions. I think he left to find his answer."

"But what *kind* of answer?" asked the boy. He really didn't understand what she was talking about. "And why did he have to leave to find it?"

"I don't know," the woman said. "I don't know why he had to leave."

Clare thought for a while, and his face slowly clouded. "He shouldn't have left," he finally said. "Who *cares* about questions like those?"

"Your father did," said the woman.

"But what about *us?*" demanded Clare, his voice rising into anger. "How could he leave without saying anything?"

His mother looked gently at her son. "Perhaps it was easiest for everyone that way."

"Not for me," the boy said, shaking his head. "He should've told me."

The woman put her hand on the back of his neck. "Someday he'll be back," she said.

They sat in silence for a few minutes. Then Clare said, "I thought he was dead." Rumors claimed that the horseman had robbed and killed his master. This was difficult to believe, though—his father's servants were remarkably devoted.

The woman smiled. "No, he's certainly alive."

"How do you know?"

She shook her head slowly. "I don't know how, really. I just know that when he finds his answer, he will return."

Clare looked across the fields to the rising northern hills. Then suddenly he announced, "I'm going to go find him."

The woman smiled at the idea. "I think that would be quite a search."

"But I'll do it," said the boy, turning back to her. "Whatever it takes, I'll find him." He recalled Mr. Tannen's stories and began to speak quickly. "I'll climb over mountains if I have to. I'll go to the sea. Whatever it takes, I'll do it."

His mother looked carefully at him. "Clare," she said, "it's really not necessary—"

"But it *is*," he insisted. "I want to find my father. He's been gone long enough—I'll bring him home."

She decided not to argue; she had seen this kind of passion in him before. "You *will* take your journey," she agreed. "It's beginning to stir in you even earlier than it did with your father. But Clare, there's something you should know."

"What's that?" he asked. His thoughts were still with the mountains.

"There's really nothing out there."

"Out where?"

"Out anywhere. In the mountains or by the sea, it's all the same—same as this garden, same as this front porch." She motioned to the hills. "There's nothing out there that isn't right here."

"My father's out there," said Clare. And then, when the woman didn't respond, he added, "And besides, even if I don't find him, I'll get to see the mountains and the sea."

"The bugs don't interest you anymore?" she asked.

He looked a bit embarrassed. "Mom, that was fine when I was a kid. But—you know—you outgrow that kind of stuff." He spoke firmly. "I need to explore. And I need to find my father."

She nodded. "I understand."

As they sat, the boy thought about the prospect of such a trip. Countless adventures, no doubt. Breathtaking new horizons. Proper challenges for a young man like himself—and no more of the boring garden work. A smile spread over his face. "There's a whole world out there," he said softly. "Mom, it's waiting to be explored. How can you say that everything's right here?"

"It's what I've learned," she said. "Your father left, I believe, to see if I was right."

The boy pivoted in his chair. "But you really think that life out there is just like life in our town?"

"No, things may seem quite different out there." She smiled. "Not everyone is as lucky as we are."

"So what are you saying, then?"

"I'm saying that there's nowhere to go. The whole world is within you, and you take it with you every step of the way. There's nothing special beyond those hills."

He shifted in his seat. "Mom," he said quietly, "how can you say that? You've lived here your whole life. You haven't been around."

"You're right," she said. "But I've found happiness right here among the simple treasures of the earth—

my plants and my child. That proves to me that there's nothing more to seek."

He slowly folded his arms. "Well, I need to go."

The woman ran her fingers through her son's tangled hair. "Your life is yours," she said. "And you may do whatever you wish." She kissed his dirty forehead and rose from her chair. The boy watched her walk off toward the garden.

∾

And thus it was decided.

Several years passed before Clare was actually ready to leave. He and his mother continued to tend the garden and sell the fruits of their labor at the marketplace—but things felt different. Now that he had decided upon a mission, Clare began to feel quite tender toward the garden. The dirt felt warm and generous between his fingers. The boring chores became like old friends. Weeding, watering, shoveling the compost heap—all grew precious as time went on.

The school years passed, each month becoming increasingly carefree as the significance of his lessons faded. Clare spent his time dreaming and wondering, planning the steps of his journey. Time meandered forward, the boy matured, and his anticipation grew steadily stronger.

When at last the day arrived he was ready. His arms rippled with light, garden-grown muscles. Across his back hung a fat burlap pack. His face was strongly set and his childhood innocence was gone. Or at least, thought his mother, watching him approach, the innocence was buried under a mound of determination. He was ready for anything, and the woman saw it. She addressed him with a tone of formality that seemed appropriate.

"Well," she said, looking him over, "everything seems to be in place."

He straightened his back, adding an inch or two to his height. He looked proud. "You know," he told her seriously, "I might be gone for a long time."

She nodded. "I understand."

"Will you be OK? By yourself, with the garden and all?"

His mother smiled. "I think so," she said.

"That's good." He didn't say anything else for a while. Then he added, "Because if you really need me here, I can probably come back soon. Maybe in a month or two."

"No," she told him, "you can take as much time as you need."

"OK." They were standing at the edge of the garden, at the point where the path from the house ended. He turned to look toward the road. It looked bigger somehow.

"Before you go," his mother said, "I want to present you with a gift."

"A gift?" He turned back to face her.

"Actually, it's a gift you already have. It's called a touchstone."

The boy looked confused.

She said, "When miners are digging for gold, they carry around with them a piece of black rock—flint or jasper, I think. If they find something that looks like gold they scrape it on the rock. Depending on the streak it leaves, they can tell if they've found real gold or fool's gold."

Clare shifted the pack on his shoulders. "You're giving me a piece of rock?" he asked.

The woman smiled. "No. I'm trying to show you a different kind of touchstone—a touchstone of truth, you could call it."

"But it's not a rock." His pack was heavy enough already.

She laughed. "No. Your touchstone is inside you, and you can use it anytime. Whenever someone you meet presents you with a new idea—and most likely, everyone will—look at the streak that it leaves in your heart. The mark left by the truth is simple, luminous, and very warm."

He considered her words and asked, "What about harsh truths? They don't leave a very warm feeling."

"Only the warm ones last," she said. "Whenever we accept a harsh idea about life, we end up finding something to replace it later on. And so we keep moving toward the ultimate truth: Life is so very wonderful. Chalk it up to our touchstones."

He nodded, searching around for his touchstone. "I'll try to use it," he finally said.

"Good. Now walk carefully, and remember to laugh when the shadows block your path." She clasped him in a long, tight embrace. Then she let him go.

He nodded and turned away. Watching him cross through the garden and sniff one last fading rose, she yielded to her contained emotion and allowed two streams to run from her eyes.

As he moved off toward the dusty road, the boy could not have been older than sixteen.

TWO

Clare stamped the ground with his first step, marking the beginning of his journey. His second step had a bit of a twist to it, and by the end of the first mile he was practically skipping along. The road felt powerfully important beneath his feet. No longer was it a boring and dusty old thing; now it was a bridge to another life.

The young man smiled at the sparrows, nodded to his vine-covered oak, and finally took leave of the road by way of a forest trail. According to a map that Mr. Tannen had given him, the northern hills climbed gradually into a high mountain range. They would serve as his first conquest.

For a good three or four days, Clare flew on the wings of his freedom. "This is *it*," he thought to himself, moment after happy moment. The boy fell asleep on the soft forest floor and was filled with a sense of peace. All his days began with unprovoked laughter. Hiking with the fat duffel strapped to his back, life simply shone.

The quiet avenue through the pines widened into an unfamiliar dirt road as he walked, and the road itself eventually became a gravelly thoroughfare. He tread upon it lightly, moving with a quick step toward his future. A week passed like this, and Clare began to chuckle. He had been a bit worried about homesickness and that sort of thing—but *this?* This was sheer joy.

At the week's end his food supply ran low, and he decided to resupply. Passing through the next small town, Clare mustered his roughest voice and said "hey" to a gentleman leaning against a wooden post. The man raised an eyebrow. "Can you tell me where I can buy some supplies around here?" asked Clare.

The man casually bounced off the post and approached him. "What do you want to buy, kid?"

"Just some food for a week," he told the man. "Maybe some rope, too." He didn't particularly appreciate the "kid" part.

"Sure," said the man, scratching the front of his red mustache with two fingers. "How much do you have to spend?"

"Not a whole lot," Clare said, a little cautiously.

The man nodded. "And tell me—what's a kid like you doing in these parts? This is pretty tough country, you know."

Clare looked around and raised his chin a bit. "I'm on a journey."

"A journey?" drawled the man, looking suddenly interested. "What kind of journey would that be?"

"I'm looking for my father," Clare told him. "He left when I was young and I haven't seen him since." He decided to leave it at that.

"And where's your father now?" asked the man. "Around here somewhere?"

The boy frowned a little. "Actually, I don't know."

"But you must have *some* idea where he is. . . . "

"Well," said Clare, "not really. But I'll find him somehow." Then he added, "I'm heading for the mountains. I'm going to start looking there."

The man began walking in a slow circle around him. He looked thoughtful. "You know," he said, "I bet I could help you out—with your journey, that is."

Now Clare began to grow nervous. His eyes darted about to see if anyone was around. "Yeah?" he laughed. "How's that?"

The man's lips opened into a grin. "Oh," he said, "I help people out all the time."

Though he tried to hide it, Clare was trembling now. He had seen this kind of game before—with Kat and her mice. Taunting, flirting, circling, then. . . . He knew he had to act at once.

"Look," he said sharply, "I'm going to find my father." Before his companion could speak, he added, "And *no* one is going to stop me."

The red-mustached man opened his mouth to say something, but Clare quickly interrupted him.

"And I *don't* need any help," he said. "I just want some supplies. Tell me where I can get some. Otherwise, go circle someone else."

The man was speechless; he pointed to a darkened storefront. As Clare turned to walk away, the man called out, "If I see him, I'll tell your ol' father you're looking for him."

The boy quickly purchased his food and hurried back onto the highway. He let out a huge sigh of relief.

Now as he walked he kept to the side of the road and avoided eye contact with the occasional passing traveler. His thoughts continued to dwell upon the red-mustached man. What could he have done if the scene had become ugly? Probably not a whole lot, he admitted. And he began to feel alone.

Clare's enthusiasm dwindled soon after that experience, and problems immediately began to crop up in its place. It rained, for example—three days in a row—and the absence of firewood collapsed his menu into nine meals of dry bread and cheese. His discouragement grew. His steps came heavier and more slowly.

One late evening, while trying to lash his tarp to a tree, Clare slipped backwards into a mud puddle. His bruised tailbone kept him up all night. Then it rained some more, drenching his remaining embers of hope.

The young traveler trudged forth now, moving at half-speed toward his goal. He began to stumble over his own questions: Why am I doing this? Where am I going? Why did I want to leave home so badly? The answers were tough to find.

Several days along this unhappy train of thought, finding himself at a relative low point, Clare lost his hat to an unannounced gust of wind. He had just walked out of a grove of trees, into an open field, when—*whoosh*. The hat was gone. He made a grab, but to no avail.

The little cap flew up and away for thirty feet or so; then it dropped to the ground. In an instant, it was back up again, tumbling away, far out of reach. Clare unloaded his pack from his shoulders and sat down. He watched the hat race toward the horizon. And then he began to smile.

A smile first; then a chuckle. This put things in perspective. The gust of wind, the blowing hat, the open road—somehow it reminded him of home, and his mother, and her story of the winds.

∽

When Clare was young, he and his mother would spend long afternoons walking through the neighboring lands. There were forests, cool and green; meadows rippling with tall, golden grasses; gentle hills upon which to scamper. Clare ran, mostly, bouncing off the trails and into the unexplored. Usually he returned to the strolling woman only when he needed to catch his breath.

For the most part she walked in silence, speaking only when there was something to say. She plucked pine cones from the trees and described the folds that captured the seeds. She found entrances to the prairie dog burrows. She saw the paw prints and traced them with a finger. Clare soaked it all up, questioning her comments, drawing new conclusions. He loved their walks together—most of all, because of the stories.

A walk with his mother was certain to bring a story or two. Some were the age-old fables of poisoned apples and sleeping princesses; others were true legends of heroes and heroines. Some were mythic, pointing a way toward the order of the world. Others were almost like riddles, or jokes. Clare loved them all. He listened with rapt attention until the tale had unwound. Then he thought about it for a while. At bedtime, he usually wanted to hear the same story again.

There were four which he held particularly dear—the tales of the four winds. His mother had invented these herself, he thought, for they carried what felt like a personal message. He once asked her where she had heard them.

"Why, from the winds, of course," she replied with a grin.

"But *how?*" he asked. "I don't hear anything from the winds."

"Ah," she said, kneeling down. "But you must listen closely. The wind speaks only in whispers." Her voice, by then, had dropped almost to nothing.

Clare whispered back, "But how? All I can hear is a big woo-oo-osh. I don't hear any *words*."

"The winds have been around the world," she told him, "and they have seen the lives of every boy, woman, and man. All year they fly about, wrapping themselves around people and carrying their conversations. The winds gather stories, and then, once a year, they all come together."

"Where?" the boy asked, still whispering. "Where do they meet?"

"I suppose they meet at the edge of their lands—where north meets south, and east meets west. There they come, once a year, to share the best of their stories. If you listen *very* carefully and *very* quietly," she continued, cupping a hand to her ear, "you can listen to them speak."

Clare cupped his hand to his ear like his mother. There, in a bright and open field, they listened.

"What are they saying?" he finally asked, keeping his hand at his ear.

"The East Wind is speaking now," his mother replied, concentrating deeply on the sound of the rustling grass. "I think it's telling a story of a man who learned to fly."

Clare dropped his hand, raising his voice excitedly. "Oh, tell me. Please—I want to hear the story."

So his mother straightened herself, wrapped her hand around one of Clare's, and began to lead him down the path. "There was once a man who was a dreamer," she began. Then turning, she said, "At least, that's what the East Wind told me. This dreamer sat around his home all day, dreaming of wonderful things to do. He dreamed of things to build and he built them.

He dreamed of songs to sing and he sang them. Mostly he built toys, and mostly he sang songs that were happy and fun. Everyone who knew the dreamer loved him—even if they *did* think he was quite peculiar.

"Now, one day this dreamer got a particularly fantastic dream stuck in his head: he dreamed that he could fly. It was a dream, but it almost felt real to him. He could *almost* feel himself soaring like the eagles. He could *almost* feel himself dancing like the butterflies. He dreamed this dream for many days. And then he decided to try it out.

"The dreamer rushed out of his house, heading straight for the village square. When he reached the center of town, he grabbed hold of a heavy rope and gave the thing a pull. This sent the town bells crying, calling all the townspeople to the square.

"When everyone in the town had arrived, the dreamer stood upon a box and announced, 'I have rung the bells because I've dreamed of a marvelous thing. I have dreamed that I can fly.'

"The people looked at each other for a moment. They started to smile. Then they began to laugh—first quietly, but then louder. After a minute or two, everyone in the town was rolling in guffaws and belly-chortles. 'Dreamer,' said one, slapping the man on the back, 'you have truly outdone yourself this time. What a terribly funny idea! Think of it—a man flying! Like the birds!' All the townspeople carried on like this for a while.

"When they had calmed down a bit, the dreamer spoke again. 'It *does* seem funny,' he admitted. 'But I dreamed it, and it must be possible. Will anyone help me learn to fly?'

"Now the people frowned. It was a humorous idea, of course, but this dreamer was *serious*. 'Dreamer,' said one, 'if we were meant to fly, don't you think that we would have been given wings?' All the people laughed at this—surely it was an obvious thing.

"But the dreamer wouldn't be deterred. 'If I can dream it, I can do it,' he said. 'Will no one help me?'

"By this point, the people had grown weary of the silly man's ideas. 'Look,' they said, 'it's impossible. You'll find that out sooner or later.' And they went back about their business.

"So the dreamer stood alone for a while in the square. He thought about ringing the bell again, to try to convince the people to help him. But he realized that no one was interested. He then walked back to his house, packed up a traveling bag, and left the town to seek a teacher.

"He walked for many days on the road until he came to another town. This town was smaller, and it housed fewer people. Though its village square was small, it had a big bronze bell and a sturdy rope. The dreamer knew what to do. Walking up to the rope, he gave the thing a pull and set the bell clanging. All the townspeople flowed out of their buildings and into the square.

"The dreamer didn't need to stand on a box this time; the group was much smaller. 'Townspeople,' he said, 'I am a visitor from far away. I have come because I want to learn how to fly.'

"The people looked at each other for a moment. They began to smile. Then they began to laugh—but not as loudly as the ones before. 'Sir,' said one, 'flying is a wonderful dream. But it is impossible. People are too heavy, and the ground is too close to our feet. Flying is not for humans.'

"The dreamer shook his head. 'I have dreamed it, and so it must be possible,' he said. 'Is there no one here who will help me?'

"Someone else stepped forward. 'Dreamer,' he said, 'there is no way to fly. But we in this town have learned to run so fast and lightly across the ground that one almost *feels* like flying. It's as close as anyone can get to the real thing. If you like, we will be happy to teach you how to run in this way.'

"So the dreamer agreed. He stayed in the town for several days, learning how to send his feet along the ground with such strength and agility that it *did* sometimes feel like flying. But it wasn't what he had dreamed. When he had learned how to run in this way, the dreamer thanked the townspeople and continued on down the road.

"After a while, he came across another town. This one was even smaller than the last, and it had only a little bell with a small piece of rope. He rang the bell. People trickled out of their homes, into the town square, to see what was the matter.

"The man looked at the small collection before him. 'Townspeople,' he said, 'I have come to your town because I want to learn how to fly. The people in my town said it was impossible. The people in the last town said it was impossible, but they taught me to run so fast that it sometimes *feels* like flying. Now I have come to you, because I have dreamed that I can truly fly. If I have dreamed it, it must be possible.'

"The people looked at each other and they began to smile. But this time they didn't laugh. 'Dreamer,' they said, 'yours is a very noble dream. We, too, wished to fly, but we have found it impossible. Our bodies are simply not designed for life in the air. However,' they added, 'we have learned to run very fast, like you. And we have also learned to listen to the wind, and measure its roving air currents. We have learned how to run very fast atop the highest hills and then jump exactly when the air currents are strong below us. In this way, we have been able to fly for a few seconds.'

"The dreamer considered their words. 'It's not the flight which I dreamed of,' he said, 'but I would like to learn this skill of yours.' So he stayed in the town for a few days, learning how to read the wind and leap off the highest hills. Several times, for a few seconds, he felt as though he was flying. But quickly he fell upon the ground. 'This is not the flight of my dream,' he finally said to the people. 'I am grateful for what you have taught me, but I must leave to find what I came for.'

"The people nodded supportively. 'True flight is impossible, except for the birds and insects,' they said. 'But we wish you the best of luck in your search.'

"The man left the town and continued down the road for many days. The land was quiet here, and villages were nowhere in sight. 'Will I have to turn back?' the man asked himself. 'Is there no one around here who knows how to fly?' But then he remembered his dream, and once again he could feel himself flying—he was weightless as a milkweed puff, happy as a blue jay. The dreamer walked on for many more days, lost in his colorful reverie.

"Finally the road moved through a wide and open field, and there, in the distance, he saw something strange.

"What it looked like was a large kite. And there was a *person* below it, dragging the thing across the ground. He walked quickly over to the place and found a woman seated upon the ground, flushed with exertion.

" 'Madam,' the dreamer began, unsure what to say, 'you appear to be having difficulties.'

"The woman sighed. 'It's *this*,' she said, waving at the giant contraption. 'I can't get it to work.'

"The dreamer looked curiously at the thing. It did indeed appear to be a giant kite—there was a wooden frame, and a wide piece of fabric covered the whole thing. It looked rather beaten by use. 'What does it do?' the dreamer asked.

"The woman sighed again. 'Oh—it probably sounds silly to you, but this thing has been a dream of mine. You see, I've always wanted to have a pair of wings. Everyone laughed a lot when I told them that, but when they finished laughing, some people were kind enough to offer a point or two of advice: how light wings need to be, how strong the bones are inside them—that kind of thing. Eventually I learned enough to build this.' She motioned at the invention. 'Sort of a giant wing. But I can't get it into the air.'

"The dreamer smiled then, and he took the woman's hand. 'May I try?' he asked. She nodded hopefully. Together they carried the wing to the highest hill, and strapped it on to the dreamer's back.

"The dreamer began to run, faster than he had ever run before; he danced his feet across the hilltop and listened carefully for the currents of air. When he reached the edge of the hill, the dreamer angled the wing into the current, leaped higher than ever before possible, and—silence. He was in flight.

"The woman let out a whoop of joy from below. 'You're flying!' she cried, racing below him. 'You're flying!' The dreamer dove and climbed for five minutes upon the currents, flying like the birds he had long dreamed about. When the winds finally died he coasted back to the ground. 'My friend,' he said, 'you have taught me two things. The first is that nothing is impossible. The second is that we *are* meant to fly.' And he spent the rest of the afternoon teaching her how to run, leap, and listen to the wind."

∾

Now, as Clare sat, watching his hat blow across the meadow, *he* listened to the wind. It was a young wind which blew here, full with the spirit of youth. It seemed to urge him onward. It whispered to him of adventure and unfolding excitement. He listened to it, watched his hat blow away, and began to grow strong in its presence.

What had his mother said after that story? "Clare, you can do anything. Don't let anyone convince you otherwise."

"Can I fly? Even that?" he had asked, his eyes wide with the possibilities.

"Even that," she had said. "Anything you want."

So here he was, out to find his father. This was his flight; nothing else really mattered. So *what* if he didn't have much to go on?

The boy strode forward, his spirits renewed. As he walked, the sun came out, left again, and then concluded its game by shining brightly for two straight weeks. The joy of the journey was back. The birds sang in his ears, the sky smiled down upon him, and once more Clare was filled with purpose.

When finally he arrived at the edge of the sprawling foothills, he plopped down within a roadside field and prepared a little picnic. "Yes, this is good," he told himself, savoring a drink from his canteen. It was then that he heard a scream.

Even though it sounded far away, Clare involuntarily clenched his teeth. Maybe it was a bird, he thought. After a few minutes, he heard it again—more like a sorrowful wail this time. He decided that it was definitely human. Clare frowned, packed his bag, and began creeping toward the sound. Moving in tandem with the highway, he soon came across the seated figure of a man.

The fellow was alone, middle-aged, and he was vigorously engaged in a conversation with himself. His head bobbed along with his stream of words, attended by a variety of gestures and poses. After ten or fifteen minutes, the man jumped up, filled the air with a mournful cry, and sat back down again.

Clare didn't know what to do. He waited and watched from the safety of the field. Then, two or three cries later, the boy crawled out and approached the man. "Hello?" he offered with upraised eyebrows.

". . . a shame it is! Oh what a shame! It really was so beautiful once. So wide and green, so soft to the fingers . . . " The man seemed not to notice his visitor. Clare stood and watched him for a few minutes, feeling rather confused.

"Hello?" he tried again.

". . . rolling beautiful lands! Perfect, really. So very perfect. Oh, where has it gone? The beautiful, wonderful lands . . . "

Clare made a last attempt. "*Hello?*" he said, placing his face within inches of the man's nose.

Now the fellow stopped and seemed to notice Clare for the first time. His head pivoted slowly upon his neck; then his eyes narrowed. "Could it be?" he muttered, studying the boy. He looked suddenly critical. "A little thin, perhaps. But—yes—perhaps." He was nodding now.

"I heard you yell," explained Clare, not particularly enjoying the examination. "Is something wrong?"

The man's jaw dropped at the question. "Wrong!" he cried. "What *isn't* wrong? Oh!" He looked as if he was about to utter another wail. "The poor kingdom! It used to be so nice."

Clare took a step back. "And what happened to it?"

The man shook his head in grief and pointed down the road. "It's almost gone. Gone, lost, ruined." Then his eyes blazed. "But you! You can bring it back!"

"Me?"

The man leaped forward and clutched the boy's shoulders. "I have been waiting for you!" he shouted. "You can help to bring back the kingdom!"

"Me?"

"Of course, yes, you—but be careful." His voice turned serious. "It's a dark and dangerous place these days. Be prepared for anything."

"Like what?" asked the concerned boy.

"*Anything,*" repeated the man ominously. "Now go on along there—no time to lose. What an important job!" He shuffled Clare on down the road. After a minute he called, "Good luck!" The boy could only shake his head at the strange meeting.

A few miles later, he came across a smattering of houses. They were old and battered, and some had

38

practically fallen down. A woman was hanging her laundry on a line in front of one of the sturdier-looking structures. Clare called out to her. "Excuse me, ma'am," he said, "but might there be a village ahead?"

"Where are you from?" she asked sharply.

"From pretty far away," came the humble response.

"Well, there's a *city* ahead," she informed him. "But I don't know of any *villages* around here." With that, she turned back to her work.

Clare continued on, somewhat shaken. Small changes worked through the character of the land as he walked: tree patches thinned into tiny collections of homes, refuse occasionally blew across the highway, and the roadside gullies began to run with a black wetness. The air took on a smelly tinge, and a disquieting energy started to unnerve the boy.

It was something about the houses, he thought. The houses were so barren, so deathly still, without a hint of a dog or a child rushing about. The brusque laundry woman was the only person who appeared to live in any of them—and she was a distance back. Clare sidestepped into the middle of the road and began to look over his shoulder.

Near the end of the day, wondering where to settle his camp, he noticed an unexpected glint of silver in the corner of his eye. Turning to examine it, his jaw met squarely with a ring-encrusted fist.

The blow was very hard; it swept all consciousness from the boy. This was actually a fortunate turn, for it allowed him to slumber away while his duffel bag, clothes, and a slight measure of flesh were cut away by three greedy knives.

After completing their work, the band of thieves shoved his body into a ditch. Twenty minutes later, two passersby shuddered at the sight and quickened their step toward the city.

If it wasn't for the full moon which rose early that night, the outline of a woman heaving Clare's body onto her donkey would hardly have been perceptible.

∾

The tone of the boy's sleep edged from a black unconsciousness into a lightening gray discomfort before finally dissolving into the pain of day. Everything in him hurt. Every part of his body ached. His waking thoughts were of home, his life, and the undeniable failure of his journey.

A sob snuck out of his belly. Then another. He couldn't hold them back; they began to roll forth like a gathering river. The loneliness he had denied, the confusion and fear of the past weeks burst from his heart. He cried for an hour, dampening the cotton bandages which swathed him. Finally the pressure of his grief subsided and he raised a weary head.

"Hello," a woman said softly. Clare turned quickly toward the voice and met with a pair of remarkably concerned eyes. "You'll be fine," she said, and he fully believed her. Without a word, the boy fell back asleep.

When Clare awoke again, a lamp was burning. The woman was still sitting in her chair. "Did you sleep better this time?" she asked.

"Yes," came a rasp from his throat.

"Good," she said. "My name is Samara, and there's some water next to your bed." He slowly slid into a sitting position and took a careful drink. Looking over the rim of his glass, he studied the woman. She was dressed in light-colored clothes and her face had a motherly kind of compassion to it. Her hair was a dusty shade of gold. Clare decided that she looked a lot like the White Witch from his book of fairy tales.

"You must not be from around here," she said. "Not too many people travel the highway at night." He shook his head in agreement.

"How did you find me?" he asked after draining the water from his glass.

"I heard about your situation," she explained. "Some people in the city know me as a healer. They keep me informed of those in need."

"Are you a doctor?" Clare asked, wondering at his tightly bound bandages.

She smiled. "Not really a doctor. More like a nurse."

"Oh."

"You're welcome to stay here for as long as you wish," added the woman, rising from her chair. "Try to rest as much as possible for the next several days." With that, she shut off the lamp and bade him a good night.

☙

The golden-haired woman came and went over the next week, presumably tending the wounds of other victims pulled from highway ditches. When Clare had regained enough strength to carry his half of a conversation, he asked her about herself.

"Samara, what is it exactly that you do?"

She sat down. Her eyes flickered in the lamplight. "I guess you could say I'm a minister."

He was confused. "I thought you were a nurse. What do you minister about?" he asked. Then, rephrasing his question, "I mean, what type of minister are you?"

She laughed. "A minister of love."

Clare had never heard of a minister of love. "Well, who do you minister *to?*" he asked.

"To anyone who will spend a little time with me," she said. "People like yourself."

He coughed. Who was this woman? And what could he do with something like *love?* He loved his mother, and the garden back home, and even perhaps his father. At least he cared enough to go find his father. He had struggled through a love affair or two in school; it seemed pretty simple to him. And anyway— he was just fine without all that. Clare shifted uncomfortably. "Well, how do you minister love?"

"What I try to do," she said, leaning back in her chair, "is show people that life *is* love. And that all our happiness lies in its arms, and all journeys lead to it. And, of course," she added, leaning forward, "everyone else shows me the same thing."

Clare bit his lower lip and then asked, "How do they do that?"

"They really can't help themselves," she said.

The boy looked around the room. He was beginning to feel quite uneasy about his situation. "Really," he said to her. "And why can't they?"

"Because love is a magical thing," she said. She brushed off his discomfort with her laughter. "Don't worry," she said. "It's not as serious as it sounds. I just wanted to explain my mission to you."

He decided that it wasn't much of an explanation. "Oh," he said.

"And I can always use a helping hand," she added, nodding. "Please consider staying here for a while."

So consider it he did. He also considered the matter of his lost money and supplies. It seemed like a good idea to stick around for a week or two.

"Samara," he explained, "I'm on a journey to find my father. He left home when I was young. That's where I was going when you found me."

"I wondered what you were doing out on the highway," she said.

"Yeah. Anyway, I need to find him. I can't stay for long. But since all my things are gone, and since I don't know anyone else around here, I guess I'd like to help you out for a few days."

"Wonderful," she nodded. "You can apprentice with me for a while, and I'll provide you with the things you need for your journey. As I said, you can stay for as long as you want."

That sounded like a reasonable plan to Clare, who had but one question. "What exactly will I do as your apprentice?"

The woman smiled mysteriously. "You'll see."

For the week and a half of his convalescence, Clare hadn't left his room. The noise outside his boarded-up window suggested that Samara lived in a busy place, but the boy knew nothing else of his surroundings. Finally, on his first day of health, he followed Samara out her front door and was promptly assaulted by a horrible vision.

Here, a piteous father and daughter begged coins from the mouth of an urban alleyway. There, a broken

43

and diseased animal crawled through a pile of garbage. The walls were tall and sooty and cramped, and the streets seeped with rivulets of grime. Clare lurched backwards in shock.

"Welcome to the city," said Samara over her shoulder. She approached the forlorn-looking couple and traded a few words with them while Clare recovered. "Come on," she waved to him. "Let's get to work."

He stumbled forward, looking blankly into the eyes of the small child. She seemed as stunned by this world as he was. "Over here!" Samara guided him from around a corner. He hurried ahead.

"I've never seen a place like this," he whispered to her, horrified.

She chuckled. "Yes, I suspected that you hadn't." They moved on. "I came here many years ago, to practice my art. This place has certainly taught me one big lesson."

Clare looked around. "What's that?"

"Before I came," she explained, "I thought I knew about love. I thought love was kindness and sensitivity."

He paused. "Well, sure."

"But since I've been here," she continued, "I've learned that kindness is only half of love. There's another half, just as important: strength. It's taken me a while to learn that."

Clare studied the woman as they walked. "You seem strong enough to me," he told her.

She nodded. "Perhaps now. Not always, though. Not when I first came here."

"And why *did* you come here?" Clare wanted to know. "You said something about your art?"

"Yes, my art." She brushed some strands of hair from her face. "When I was a young child, the world frightened me terribly—I worried about everything imaginable. Things like sickness, war, and hunger. It all seemed so overwhelming."

The boy nodded. "I guess it *is* overwhelming if you think about it too much."

"It was for me. I wanted to end the problems in the world. I wanted to end all the suffering. And so I tried to be extra sensitive to everyone's pain. If someone was hurting, I hurt too."

"It sounds like a noble way of living." He was impressed by the woman's commitment.

"Noble, perhaps," she said. "But it didn't work."

"No?"

"No. It didn't help anyone. I was taking the wrong approach."

The boy looked confused. "Well, I don't see what other approach there is," he said. "I mean, if you want to help someone, you need to be sensitive to their problems."

"Sure," said the woman. "But if you *really* want to help, you can't stop there. A true healer rises above it all."

Clare shook his head. "I don't understand what you mean."

"There's a lot of suffering in the world," said Samara. "Especially in the city. A lot of miserable lives."

"Yeah, so it seems."

"I've learned two ways to approach it," said the woman. Then she paused. "Well, perhaps three—the third being ignorance." She motioned to the bodies on the street. "It's pretty tough to ignore it all, though."

The boy nodded. "So what are the two ways?"

"The first is to join it," she said. "Join suffering wherever you see it. Share the pain of a hungry child, feel it, do your best to understand it. That's how I spent most of my life."

"But that way didn't work, you said."

"No. It didn't help anyone. I was constantly worn out and drained. I had nothing to give."

"Well, then what's the other way?"

"The other way is to join it and *release* it. Join it, like the first, but release it at the same time. The release is what takes strength."

"Release it to what?"

Samara smiled. "To a solution."

Clare shook his head, not quite following her. "I guess I'd have to see it," he said.

"You will," said the woman. "In the meantime, let me tell you about Nancy. She's the one who taught me about strength." Samara paused to recollect. "I first came to the city to help. Goodness knows, there was a whole lot to be done here. I arrived filled with good intentions, ready to join the ranks of the suffering.

"It turns out," she continued, "that I didn't last very long. The city was just too much to handle. Toward the end of one particularly difficult day I came across a group of men harassing a boy. He must have been about your age. Maybe they were after his money—who knows—but when I arrived, they were tossing him around. It was so frightening, that scene, that I just couldn't hold back. I screamed at them to let the boy go. I told them to leave, but they only laughed at me. I felt so powerless. It was then that Nancy showed up.

"Nancy was a short woman, shorter than me, and she was the most determined-looking soul I'd ever seen. She marched right up to that pack of wolves— very calmly, really—and told the biggest one that he'd better let her son go. Not a single muscle trembled. She just said, '*Let—my—son—go,*' very slowly, and it was like a lion talking to a mouse. The big ogre laughed nervously and shoved the boy in her direction, and then he shuffled away uncomfortably. It was unbelievable! The other men slinked away like the first. When they were gone, she introduced herself and thanked me for yelling. She said that it brought her out of her home.

"Now, I couldn't believe it. I mean, here she was, a woman this high," Samara said, holding her hand in the air, "fending off a gang of brutes all by herself. I knew she had something to teach me."

"About strength?"

"Yes, about strength. And about healing. As I was helping her bandage her son later that day, she turned to me and said, 'You want to know the secret? *Just don't make it real.*' That's all—it sounded really cryptic at the time. I asked her what she meant. She told me, 'There's only one way out of a bad situation, and that's to stop believing in it. Don't make it real, and it disappears.' She had such a sparkle in her eye when she said it. I was intrigued."

"But that doesn't make any sense," said Clare. "I mean, things don't disappear if you ignore them."

"Right. But this isn't about ignoring things. Earlier you asked me about my art—well, my art is healing, and Nancy has been my greatest teacher. She has taught me to look at the horrors of the world without believing in their reality. That's how I've learned to help."

Clare was a bit taken aback. "Honestly," he said, considering her words, "it sounds to me as if you're fooling yourself. You can't overlook things like hunger and pain. I mean, they *do* exist. Especially here."

"Sure they exist. But the important question is, Are they real?"

"How could they *not* be?" he said.

The woman thought for a minute. "Let me ask you this," she said. "When you were a child, did you ever scrape your knee? Or get stung by a bee?"

"Well, sure," said the boy.

"And did your mother kiss the hurt and make it go away?"

Clare laughed. "Yeah, I guess. Mom's kisses were magic."

"Well, that's exactly what I do," said Samara with a smile. "I give people little kisses."

Clare scratched his head. He didn't see what bee-sting kisses had to do with anything. "Well, that's a nice job you have," he said, shrugging.

She laughed. "Yes, it is. The point is that your mother's kiss worked because she refused to believe that a scraped knee was all that bad. She knew that things were OK. She knew that you'd heal—and she communicated that to you through the kiss."

"But the kiss only made me feel comforted. It didn't really *do* anything."

"But it did," insisted Samara. "It did exactly what it intended to do—it helped you out of your problem. That's the power of love. And that, I believe, is what we all seek. Just a moment of love."

"You think that that's all it takes to heal a person? Love?"

"I do," she nodded. "A person, a city, a world—that's all."

The boy didn't say anything. They walked on in silence for a while, taking care to evade the creeping sewer discharge. A brown rat scampered across their path and stared at them for a moment before disappearing. Clare began to feel slightly nauseous, and wondered dubiously at the smells in the air.

"We're needed here," Samara finally said, stopping at an unmarked door. She rapped twice and waited for a reply. After a moment, the door was opened by a hunched old woman. "Oh, Samara," she cried in relief. "Thank you so much for coming. He just won't see anyone else."

"Glad to be of service," Samara replied with a grin.

The woman gave her a hug. "Please come in," she said.

They entered into a hovel of a house, where a man sat shivering by a glowing fire. His skin was very pale. "Good to see you, Joe," greeted Samara.

"Thank you for coming." The old mouth cracked, wrinkling into a slight smile. "I thought that this might be the end."

"Not until you're ready," she assured him. She then asked the man to rise from his chair, and to Clare she instructed, "Your job is to stand behind Joe and catch him as he falls." The boy was confused, but took his place. Samara then faced the old man, closed her eyes for a moment, and spoke a few quiet words.

"By your faith you are healed," she said, or something to that effect. And as her voice left her lips, she touched Joe's forehead. The man fell gently backwards into Clare's arms, and the boy raised a pair of frightened eyes.

"It's all right," the woman assured her apprentice. "You can lay him down on the ground." Clare did so, and watched to see if the body would revive. A smile was on the old man's sleeping face; his skin gradually began to acquire a rosy flush. "He'll start to feel better as soon as he rises," Samara counseled the woman. "You know what to do if there are any problems."

The hunched tenant wrapped her arms about Samara, hugging her with a surprising strength. "It's tough to have faith, sometimes, when they're so close," the woman said. Samara nodded in agreement.

"Who *are* you?" demanded Clare when they were back outside.

"I told you," she smiled. "A minister, a healer."

"But you just touched that guy and he collapsed. How did you do that?"

"He believed I could," she explained as they walked through the narrow streets. "And so did I. That's the strength I spoke of before. It's just faith."

"What?" he exclaimed. "You're telling me you're a *faith* healer?"

"I guess you could call me that if you wanted," she considered with a look of mild amusement, "although you seem pretty surprised by the idea."

They went through the routine three other times that day. None of the other people were as old as Joe, but all were certainly as ill. One had a pain in his chest, one was sick with pneumonia, and another had a broken leg that wouldn't mend. All collapsed with a smile into Clare's arms and were gingerly laid upon the ground. By day's end, the boy's disbelief had begun to dissipate.

"So," he hesitatingly asked her, "when exactly did you get this power of yours?"

"Clare," grinned the woman, "this is love we're talking about. It doesn't belong to me or to anyone else. It's everywhere, just waiting to be used."

"Well, no one is going to tip over backwards if *I* touch them."

"Have you tried?"

"Of course not. But I'm not about to, either. I think the whole thing is pretty strange." He shook his head. "I mean, how can words—or love, as you say—heal someone? It's impossible."

"But you've seen it," she said.

"I've seen a few people fall over. That's all."

Samara laughed. "No, I mean you've seen it lots of times before. Love is what works through your mother's kisses—or even through your doctor's medicine. It's not so strange really."

"It *is* strange. At least, to watch you do it, it is." He frowned at her. "So you think you can just pop anyone back to health? Even people with really bad problems?"

"I can't," said Samara. "But love certainly can."

"Anyone?" asked Clare. He was thinking about the man he had met on the way to town.

"Sure, but love must be welcomed. It's the sick person who decides when—and how—to accept it. Try to see it for yourself," she suggested. "The next time you're sick, notice when your health begins to turn around. I bet that it will happen as soon as you're ready to reach out to someone. Here, have you heard the story of the king and the ghost?"

"No," said Clare, shaking his head.

"It's a tale that has been around these parts for a while. If I remember correctly, it goes something like this: Once there was a king who loved to ride around his kingdom in a carriage. He would wave at all the people he passed and fill his sight with his kingdom's beautiful lands. His only companion on these trips was his carriage driver, whom he trusted very much.

"One day while the king was riding through a local marsh he caught sight of something mysterious from the corner of his eye. However, when he turned to look at it, nothing was there. 'Did you see something move over in that direction?' he asked his driver, pointing to the spot. The driver politely shook his head. It happened again, and then again: every few minutes, the king would see a flicker of motion, but when he turned his head to investigate, the thing was gone.

"By the end of his trip the king was very disturbed. He wondered if his vision was failing him. As the carriage reached the far edge of the marsh, the king resolved to catch sight of whatever it was that was plaguing him. Quickly he wrenched his head backward, and for an instant he saw it: a ghostly gray cloud, which instantly vanished. He cried out in shock and fear, and the driver turned to see what was the matter. 'There!' cried the king. 'Did you see it? A marsh ghost!' The driver shook his head slowly; he had seen nothing.

"When they arrived back at the castle, the concerned driver suggested that perhaps the king had come down with a fever due to the cool marsh air; perhaps, said the driver, he had simply been hallucinating. The king nodded in agreement and immediately went to bed. His heart was troubled, though, for he *knew* what he had seen. Throughout the night he dreamed of marsh ghosts and feverish carriage trips. He also dreamed of losing his kingdom due to the charge of insanity. When he awoke, he did indeed feel feverish and confused. 'Leave me alone,' he told all his visitors. 'I am not well.'

"And so it went for many weeks. The king, thinking he was going mad, refused to speak to anyone. 'Surely even a *fool* knows that ghosts don't exist,' he thought. 'It's only a matter of time before they realize I'm mad—and then I will lose my throne.' As the king dwelled upon these ideas, his condition steadily worsened.

"Finally, a wise old healer persuaded the carriage driver to explain what had happened during the carriage ride. She smiled when she heard the story; then she promised the driver that she would help the king. It took a while, but eventually she gained entrance to the king's chambers.

"The king was in a pitiful condition when she found him, weak and wasted away by fever. He barely stirred at her entrance. But he quickly sat upright when she asked, 'Do you know anything of ghosts, sire?'

"His eyes burned with the fever. 'Ghosts?' he said in a hoarse voice. The king then turned away, struggling with something within his heart. At long last he dropped his head and whispered, 'Yes, you must know of my condition. I have seen a ghost in the marsh to the west.'

"She spoke mysteriously. 'Ah, but sire, was it shapeless and formless? And did it vanish when you looked at it closely?'

"The king picked his head up now, his eyes filled with wonder. 'Why, yes,' he replied. 'Yes—yes! That was exactly it!' He jumped out of bed, and rushed over to her. 'What does this mean? Does it truly exist? Am I not mad?'

" 'Ah,' she said again, 'Your Majesty, you are truly blessed. The thing that you saw was the Spirit of the Marsh. It appears only to those who are destined to become great and prosperous rulers. You should thank your lucky stars that you have seen such a thing; other men seek it for their entire lives.'

"The king could not help but let out a whoop of relief. 'This is wonderful news!' he cried, hugging his visitor with newfound strength. 'Here,' he begged, 'please sit with me and tell me more of this Great Spirit.' So she did for the rest of the afternoon, and by the time that the dinner bells rang, the king was fully alive with joy and good health."

Samara nodded her head happily at the end of the story.

Clare laughed. "But you're not telling me that people get sick because they see ghosts."

"No, not literally. But when they reach out to someone willing to help, they find that their sickness is no more tangible than marsh gas. Who knows what the king really saw? Who knows what the cause is for every particular ailment? It doesn't matter, because all healing comes when ghosts are put in the proper light."

"And that light is love, you say," finished Clare somewhat uncertainly. "Whatever *that* is."

The woman nodded, grinning at the boy.

"Samara," asked Clare quietly after several long minutes, "will you teach me about this love of yours?"

She clasped an arm around his shoulder. "I hope that I've already begun."

∾

That night, the pair sat down to a pot of chamomile tea.

"You know," admitted Clare, fumbling a bit with his teacup, "I still don't understand how this works." He took a sip and put the cup down. "I mean, I *did* see it. But I don't understand. You can't really fix broken bones with love. You can't *feed* people with it."

"It's like Nancy said," explained Samara. "If you want to help anyone, you have to *not* believe in their problem. By overlooking it, you can offer a moment of hope. And that's what it takes to heal—a moment of hope, or faith, or love. Call it what you like."

"So you think that things like broken legs and hunger aren't real."

"They're certainly real for the people who believe in them," said Samara. "And that includes most of us. But are they real in a permanent sense? Of course not. If they were, healing would be impossible."

Clare shook his head, reflecting on her words. "You know, it's quite an attitude you have."

"It's not so strange, really. Think of a doctor, for example: if a patient comes to a doctor with a broken leg, does the doctor sit around and feel sorry for the patient?"

"Maybe a little," said Clare.

"Not if she's a good doctor," said Samara. "If she's good, she looks beyond the pain. She'll acknowledge it, but then she looks beyond. She *knows* the leg will be healed. She *knows* she can help. It's that confidence which helps the patient—without it, the medical techniques would do nothing."

"But you need the techniques," Clare insisted. "You need *some* kind of technique, at least."

Samara smiled. "Maybe you do. But a few good words can do the trick."

∾

"Look," said an exasperated Clare several days later, "don't you ever get *upset?* I can't believe you're so happy in the midst of all this mess." He and Samara had spent their time wandering through the city streets, speaking with old acquaintances and strangers between sessions of healing.

Clare noticed that Samara approached the most unlikely types of people—lunching businessmen, vagrants, jubilant children, and crotchety adults alike. Each point of contact added a thread to her web of warmth. All that she asked of anyone was a name, a smile, and a cordial farewell. She made it look easy to find friends in the city.

"Yes," she admitted. "I sometimes get upset. But it passes quickly. As soon as I communicate with someone, my problems vanish."

"You certainly communicate with enough people," Clare noted.

She laughed. "I discovered a while ago that communicating love is the only worthy activity in the world."

"Why do you say that?"

"Well," she explained, "here's my theory. It's a little on the abstract side." She waved to a wide-eyed child as they walked. "In this world, we're all split off from each other. We're split into bodies, separated by space. Right?"

"Sure, I guess," he shrugged.

"Well, I think we naturally belong in a state of unity, together as one. Communicating love brings us closer to this state. Blocking communication with things like anger or fear or guilt keeps us apart. And we feel sad—or get sick—simply because we feel alone."

"Hold on," protested Clare. "You said that communication is the only 'worthy activity.' What about doing something like building a house or planting a garden? Aren't those worthy activities?"

"Of course they are," she agreed. "If they're done from a spirit of love, they exist as wonderful vehicles for its communication. Then again, if those houses or gardens are created out of anger, or from a sense of fear or guilt, they probably won't do much to heal the world."

"But there are other ways to help," he insisted. "A person doesn't have to walk through the streets talking to everyone he meets, right?"

"Of course not," she grinned. "But it can certainly help."

∽

At Samara's suggestion, Clare began to approach strangers on the sidewalks. "It's part of being a minister's apprentice," she insisted. Most ignored the boy or met his advances with a scathing glance. After a long two days, he became disillusioned with the whole thing and expressed his frustration to her.

"I can't do this. No one ever talks back to me. They've probably heard about you and your grand old love; that's why you can communicate with people."

"Do you want to know what I think?" she asked.

"What?" He was pouting at this point.

"I think that they're picking up on your fear. If it's not in your voice, it may be in your eyes or your posture. Or in the scent of your skin. When you can communicate without fear, no one will refuse your offer." She added, "I'm still working on it, too."

"What's there to be afraid of?" he asked, turning away. "I'm not all that afraid."

"I think that *all* our fears are tied to the fear of communication. Deep down, we're terrified of reaching out. It's not fun to be alone, but sometimes it's even scarier to join together. We're so afraid of getting lost somehow."

"So why are *you* so skilled at it? Aren't you afraid, too?"

"Yes, I am," she replied. "But I've been working on it for a while. Here," she said, "let me tell you a story that has kept me going at times."

Clare kicked a broken bottle. "Go ahead."

"The story is about a knight in shining armor," she began. "Now, I had some trouble identifying with that type of character, but I suppose that it will be easier for a young man like you." She undercut his mood with a wink, and continued. "This knight began studying swordplay when he was but a boy. You see, knights were very respectable in that society, and the child decided early that he wouldn't rest until he was a full liege of the king. At age twelve, he began training with a featherweight rapier. By the time he was eighteen he had worked himself up to a huge two-handed broadsword. He always carried the weapon with him, and was ever alert. He even slept with one hand on its hilt." She paused to build a sense of drama.

"Go on," Clare requested.

"Well, this young swordsman began to cut down the beasts of the land. He killed two chimeras, a gorgon, and a host of other monsters whose names I have forgotten. Before long, the king honored him with a knighthood. Our swordsman grew old in the employ of his majesty, slaying over one hundred enemies in armed combat. When he finally decided that there was no one in the kingdom who could best him, he married and retired to a small tract of land. He mounted his great sword above the mantel of his new home—for it, too, deserved an honorable retirement.

"There was a problem, though. Our retired knight soon discovered that he couldn't rest without his weapon. When he finally fell asleep that first night, he dreamed of being avenged by all his former opponents. By two o'clock in the morning, the blade was back in his bedroom.

"Now, his wife was an understanding sort, and agreed to the third party's presence under one condition: that he must gradually move the sword back downstairs to the mantel. Even if a day brought only a fraction of an inch's progress, he was required to make the effort. It took him a month before he could sleep with the weapon out of arm's reach. Years passed before it left the bedroom. Only on the night of his death did he finally consent to having the sword remounted above the fireplace. The end."

"Great," Clare decided, shaking his head. "Nice life."

"I see us all in that story," Samara said, ignoring his afterword. "We all have our weapons to keep everyone away—our sarcasm, our arrogance, our petty grudges. And," she continued, "we're all terrified to let them go. We've used them for years to fight, and now we know only of a hostile world."

"It *is* a pretty hostile world."

"But here's the secret: the sword of attack is always held backwards. We think that we're holding the handle, swinging our blade at the world. In truth, though, we're gripping the blade and waving about a harmless handle. The harder we fight, the deeper we cut ourselves."

Clare sighed. "And so we should just drop our weapons. That's what you're saying?"

"Only as we're ready," she said. "The idea of leaving them all behind at once is probably too frightening. There's no rush, but we can see the goal—all we want is a peaceful day, and a good night's rest. And no one can rest with their hand on a blade."

"So it's going to take a while."

Samara smiled. "It's a wonderful journey. It gets better every day."

The boy looked closely at her. "I guess I'll trust you on that."

∾

He remained with the woman for many weeks, catching falling bodies and developing an openness of communication. Samara's singleness of purpose gave the young man support. Inspired by her affirmations, he felt himself stepping away from his own defenses: a puffed-up chest, a gruff tone of voice, knotted eyebrows, and a clenched jaw. He truly began to soften. When the woman felt satisfied with his progress, she decided that it was time for him to leave the city.

"I suggest that you spend some time with my friend Jing," she said one day. "He'll help you to continue your journey."

"Who's Jing?" Clare asked.

"A teacher," was all she would allow. "Just follow the river upstream for a few days. You'll run into him."

Clare gratefully accepted a new set of travel gear from the woman. A tailor friend of hers had sewn together several sets of clothes and a bold-looking cloak. In addition, he was given a new backpack, boots, and several weeks worth of food.

"Thank you," Clare said in parting. He gave her an awkward hug. "I'll come visit you on my way back."

She flashed one last smile. "Have a wonderful trip. And remember, never miss an opportunity to join hands."

With a quick step, he left the city.

THREE

"Wooo!" cried Clare as he set his first foot outside the city. He couldn't help himself. The air tasted so much better here. *This* summer land was green instead of gray, and he could see more than a meager patch of sky. Ah, the sky! He had forgotten how enormous it was. The reacquaintance was sweet, and the boy laughed out loud.

Clare whistled as he walked along the edge of a stream, his new boots leaving a trail in its banks. He stomped forward, snatching together the pieces of a melody, flailing dramatically at an occasional mosquito. He was glad. Sure, he missed Samara a bit, but his life was *his* again, free of the city's buildings and unfriendly humans. As he walked, a rush of freedom flowed through his mind, endlessly renewed and refreshed.

Then, abruptly, he stopped and kicked a loose stone. "Darn," he muttered to himself. For he had just remembered the story of the South Wind. It was a story like the ones Samara told; he wished he had remembered it in time to share it. Perhaps on the way back, he decided.

The story of the South Wind was a story of magic. Magic and healing, that is. Here's how his mother had told it:

In the deep southern lands, on the edge of the sea, was a little town that the South Wind loved to visit. The town was quite a lively place, for trading ships came into port there. The ships brought all sorts of interesting things: spices and clothing, new inventions and sparkling gems. The South Wind was a curious type which usually managed to wrap itself up in everyone's business.

One day, a particularly large ship sailed into the moorings. The townspeople had seen it approaching; now they were gathered around the shore. Dockhands anchored the boat. Everyone watched curiously.

For a while, nothing happened—the boat didn't even seem to have a crew. The townspeople began to talk among themselves. "Strange, isn't it?" they asked, and "Who could be inside?" Suddenly there was a flash of light and a puff of smoke, and a man appeared on the highest deck.

"People," he boomed to them in a loud and resonant voice, "you are very fortunate! I have been sailing in my ship for many, many years. I have escaped serpents and dragons to reach you. But finally I have come! Finally I have come to share my magic!"

The people of the town raised their eyebrows at the address. Who was this strange fellow? "Sir," called the town mayor, smiling, "you are welcome here, as all our visitors are. But we have outgrown magic, just as we have outgrown dragons and sea serpents."

"We shall see!" cried the man, and then he was gone from the deck. In a minute or so, he appeared among the dockside crowd. "People," he announced to the surprised faces, waving his hands as he spoke, "in my ship I have a supply of rare and beautiful beans. These beans are valuable for their appearance alone, but there is something more. These beans are of *pure magic*. They are guaranteed to heal any pain or sickness in your life." He bowed deeply. "And I personally guarantee each and every one."

Slowly the townspeople began to buzz. Surely this man was exaggerating his claims, they decided, but what if there *was* a bit of truth to what he promised? Magic or not, a cure was a cure. Nothing else seemed to help this hurt knee or that headache—why not try a magic bean? Who knows what could happen?

Before things could get out of hand, the mayor cleared his throat. "Magician," he said, addressing the man, "you may sell your beans in our town, just as any bean merchant might. But," he added sternly, looking now at the townspeople, "we in this town do *not* believe in magic."

"Agreed," said the magician. "I will set up my shop tonight."

The mysterious magician allowed no one but himself to unload his ship. All through the night, he carried box after box from the ship to a vacant storefront. In the morning, under a sign reading MAGIC HEALING BEANS, his doors finally opened.

For a while people passed by curiously; no one wanted to be the first to enter. But eventually an old man hobbled into the shop. His body was bent under the weight of his age and he leaned heavily upon an old wooden cane. "Magician," he said, "I have tried everything to straighten my back. Everyone tells me that it's no use, though—they say I'm just too old. I'm willing to try one of your beans."

The magician swirled out from behind the counter and kneeled before the man. Then he pulled out a measuring tape and began to mumble calculations to himself.

"Sir," he said at last, rising, "I have exactly the bean for you. It was invented by an old wizard for a problem just like yours." He reached into a wooden barrel and pulled out a bright pink bean. "My special back-straightening bean. I promise that it will work—in fact, I'll give you this one for free."

"Do I just chew it?" asked the old man, accepting the thing.

"Yes. Try it now," said the magician. "It will begin to work at once."

The man popped the bean into his mouth and chewed upon it slowly. "Tastes good," he admitted. "Now what's supposed to happen?"

"Well," said the magician, "different people have different reactions. But generally, a person of your age and constitution will begin to feel a little bit of a bounce in his arms. Do you feel anything yet?"

The old man felt around himself. "Not yet."

"How about now?" he asked after a few seconds. "A little bounce, maybe?"

"Maybe," said the old man slowly. "Yes, maybe just a little bit of bounce in the arms. And what else happens?"

"Ah, well, of course there is the toe tapping. But that only happens in subjects who are particularly quick to heal."

"You mean, my toes will begin to tap?"

"Just a little. Maybe one toe. Just once or twice."

They waited for a minute or two. "Hey!" shouted the old man. "I think I felt one! I think my toe moved!"

"Sir," said the magician with a bow, "you are obviously a remarkable healer. By sundown today you will be able to lay down your cane."

The old man was very excited. "Magician, this is wonderful. Will I need any more of these beans?"

The magician looked thoughtful. "For someone of your nature, I'd think that one a week would be enough."

"Great," said the old man. "I'll buy enough for a year."

The magician shook his head benevolently. "Sir— for you, it will be my gift. A year's supply of health for free." He gave the man a package of the pink beans.

For the next few minutes, there was a commotion in the street outside the magician's shop. Everyone wanted to hear the old man's story. The town baker, who happened to be walking by, caught a piece of the tale. "Old man," the baker said, stopping to ask the question, "are you saying that this magician gave you his beans for free?"

The old man nodded. "He was so sure they would work. And you know, I already feel better than I have in years."

"Do you think that he could help my shoulder? It's been bothering me for a month now."

"I bet his beans could heal anything," said the old man proudly.

So the baker entered the shop. "Magician," he said, "I don't know what I think about magic. But your beans seemed to have helped the old man out there. I'm willing to try one for my shoulder. And don't worry— I'll pay you for them."

"Certainly," said the magician. "Now, when did your shoulder begin to cause you trouble?"

The baker thought for a while. "I guess it hap-pened right around the time that I opened my second bakery. I must have pulled a muscle when I was setting up the store."

"Hmm," said the magician, thinking deeply. "I think I have just the thing for you." From his barrel he counted out ten black beans. "These will take away all your shoulder pain. But there is one thing that you must do."

"What's that?" asked the baker.

"Well, in order for these beans to work, you must sit down and rest for ten minutes of every hour. Otherwise, the beans won't be digested properly."

"Ten minutes!" cried the baker. "Do you know how much work I'd lose?"

"That is what it takes," said the magician firmly. "It's powerful magic, but you must treat it properly."

"Fine," the baker grumbled. "I'll try them for a week." He paid the magician and left with his ten black beans.

No one else came into the shop that day; they were all waiting to see how the first cases turned out.

Early the next morning, the townspeople were awakened by a cry.

"Wake up! Wake up, everyone!" shouted a voice from the street. The people sleepily opened their doors and found the old man dancing in his underwear. "It worked!" he cried. "The beans worked!" He shuffled up and down the sidewalk. "See? No cane!" Within a minute, the town was in an uproar.

The mayor called an emergency morning meeting, which everyone attended. "People," he said to the audience, "surely we cannot believe in magic. Magic is the stuff of children. But this magician fellow does indeed seem to have a powerful form of medicine. Perhaps we can try it out—but please, don't expect too much!"

This was all the people needed to hear; they immediately flocked over to the magician's shop. "Magician," they called, banging on the door. "Let us in! We want to buy your beans!"

After a few minutes, the door opened. "Welcome," said the magician, bowing his head. "Welcome, people. I have enough beans for all of you. Please, no shoving. Let everyone line up in an orderly fashion, and I will attend to each and every one of your problems."

Throughout the day, the magician sold his beans. There were red beans for sore throats, dotted ones for a fever, blue ones for poor eyesight, and white ones for broken bones. The magician seemed to have a bean for every ailment; not a single person was turned away. Some he gave special instructions. Most he simply gave beans.

Over the course of the following day, everyone asked each other a single question: "How do you feel?" In the morning, only a couple of proud souls reported a positive change in health. The numbers grew, however, until by afternoon every person in the town claimed *some* gain over their suffering. The people were quite elated.

"Magic beans!" said the innkeeper. "Who would have believed it?"

"Whatever works," said the cook. "Goodness knows, nothing else helped my leg."

"How's your digestion?" asked the tailor.

"Perfect," replied the grocer, rubbing his belly. "Finally I can eat whatever I want."

And so it went, throughout the day. There were some minor incidents, of course: two men almost came to blows over one particular misunderstanding. Eventually they decided to let the magician settle it.

"Magician," said the first, bursting into the shop. "You told me that orange beans cured swollen knuckles. But this fool here says that you sold him *green* beans for his knuckles."

"You did!" said the second. "Tell him! Green beans are what you need for swollen knuckles. Not *orange* ones."

The magician jumped out from behind his counter. "Gentlemen!" he cried. "Please, let me explain. When choosing the beans, one must take into account the different metabolism rates. One must compare the skeletal structures and the differing complexions. This is why *you* received orange beans," he said to the first, "and *you* received green beans. Trust me. It is an ancient and difficult art."

"Oh," the men nodded slowly. They were satisfied with this. Arms around each other's shoulders, they left the shop in peace. The magician sighed to himself in relief.

Time moved on in the little town; ships came and went, and the people were quite happy. Within a month of the magician's arrival, every trace of sickness and pain had vanished. There were no more aches to be found, no more coughs and no more flu. No one doubted the magic beans any longer; even the mayor himself kept a daily supply.

All was fine until the day the baker returned. "Magician," he said, "those beans worked really well on my shoulder. But I ran out last week. I want to buy some more."

The magician nodded. "Certainly. Now, which beans were those?"

"The black ones," replied the baker. "You gave me ten."

"Ah, yes," said the magician, "the black ones." He mumbled to himself as he rustled through his barrel. Then his head popped up. "Actually, I should say that you need some purple beans now. Too many black beans are bad for the blood."

"No," said the baker, shaking his head. "The black beans worked. I want them again."

"Aha," laughed the magician, a little nervously this time. "Baker, I must admit to you that I've run out of black beans. But please try these purple beans. I guarantee that they will work."

"What?" cried the baker, suddenly clutching his arm. "You have no more black beans? I *need* those beans. I can feel my shoulder starting to hurt again already."

The magician slid some purple beans across the counter. "Here—I promise. These are even better than the black ones."

The baker was fuming at this point; he scattered the purple beans with the back of his hand. "What are you trying to pull here?" he demanded threateningly. "We all know that purple beans are for stubbed toes. Are you trying to trick me?"

Now the magician *really* began to grow nervous, for this baker was quite a big fellow. He racked his brain for a solution. He mentally inventoried his ship.

He made some calculations, and finally he decided to take a risk.

"Listen," said the magician in a low voice, looking around the shop. "Can I share a secret with you?" He leaned toward the baker and whispered, "The truth is that none of these beans are magic—they're all just candy. There's really no such thing as a magic bean."

"WHAT?" bellowed the baker so loudly that the whole town came running. He grabbed the magician by the shirt. "This fellow," he cried to the gathering crowd, "tells me *there's no such thing as a magic bean!* He says that we've been eating *candy.* Can you believe it, people? We've been swindled!"

Now the people cried out. "Sink his ship!" "The magician's a fake?" "Run him out of town!"

But the magician waved his hands. "People!" he shouted desperately. "People, let me explain!" When they had quieted down a bit, he began. "People, I've given you everything you wanted. Each one of you has come to me with a pain or problem. Is there anyone here who hasn't been healed?"

The people muttered among themselves. No, they admitted, there was not a single one of them who hadn't been healed. All their aches and pains were gone.

"And did everyone get his or her money's worth?" he asked.

Yes, the people supposed, it was worth every penny to be healthy.

"And now," said the magician with a bow, "I give you the true source of magic. I give you yourselves."

"And what does *that* mean?" growled the baker.

"The beans weren't magic," the magician quickly explained. "Nothing is magic except your beliefs.

"People," he then cried, "you believed in the beans and you believed in me. *That's* the source of true magic. And now you don't need me or my beans anymore, for you see that you can have perfect health without us." And in a flash of light and a puff of smoke the magician was gone.

The South Wind saw the whole thing happen; it saw the magician drop a little smoke pellet on the ground and sneak out the back of his shop. It saw the man rush down to his ship while everyone thought about what he had said. The wind watched him set his sail, and then it gently blew him away toward other destinations.

And from that day forth, there was never a trace of pain or sickness to be found in that little town by the sea.

"And that," said Clare's mother, "was the story the South Wind told the others."

"The beans weren't magic?" asked the boy.

"No, they weren't. But the people didn't need magic beans after all."

"Well," said Clare after a moment of consideration, "*I'd* still like to find a magic bean."

His mother smiled. "Perhaps you will," she said. "Perhaps someday you will."

∾

Clare remembered that he had searched the vines for weeks after hearing that story. He didn't know exactly what a magic bean looked like, but he was sure he'd recognize it. He finally gave up after cracking open a few hundred pea pods.

Now he chuckled to himself and the memory faded. Magic beans? What a funny thought. Clare turned his attention back to the riverbank. Things were very pleasant here. The stream babbled in a happy sort of way—it sounded like laughter to his ears. The forest was deep and comforting. Clare ducked beneath low-hanging branches, bounced over half-submerged rocks, and smiled at the occasional turtle. It was a fun trip.

After four or five days of boisterous stomping, though, he began to wonder a bit at Samara's words. Didn't she say to go "a few days" upstream? And who was this Jing fellow, anyway?

Clare's moment of concern passed away with the realization that his food stocks were secure and the river he was following apparently drained from the mountains. He smiled when he thought of the mountains. What would the view be like from the top? Maybe there would be snow. Or waterfalls. The prospects kept him entertained for hours.

But after another four or five days of somewhat unenthusiastic stomping, he began to get frustrated. Where was this Jing guy? He hadn't seen anyone since he left Samara. And hey, he thought, who was Samara to tell him where to go? She was a neat person, but when was the last time *she* had walked up this way? Clare began to grumble a bit to himself as he continued forward. He decided that the highway, given all its dangers, may have been preferable to hiking along a mosquito-infested river. He tightened his brow and continued forward.

A full sixteen days from his city departure, Clare finally slammed his duffel to the ground. "Hey!" he shouted, scattering a group of birds. "I've had enough!

I'm not spending my life looking for some crazy river man!" Muttering to himself about the foolishness of following someone else's travel plans, he ripped the heel from a loaf of bread. He chomped on it in silence for a few minutes. Then, when he had finished, he secured his bag and began the long walk back toward the city.

"Leaving so soon?" came a voice from behind him. Clare turned to face a man. The character was middle-aged, and his eyes sparkled with merriment. He was obviously amused. Clare wasn't.

"No. Don't tell me," the boy instructed with an outstretched hand. "You must be Jing."

"Yes," the man laughed. "And who are you?"

"My name is Clare," he told the man. "My friend Samara told me to look for you. She said go *a few days upstream,* and it's been more than two weeks. I don't even know how to get back from out here." He looked around. "And where are we, anyway? Is this where you live?"

"I live where I am," said the man.

Clare blinked. "Well, what does that mean? And why didn't Samara say 'go two weeks upstream'? That, at least, would have made things a little easier."

"Perhaps a few days was all you needed," the man suggested. He carried a bit of mirth in his voice, as if barely containing a secret.

"Well, what's *that* supposed to mean?" said Clare. "A few days was all I needed for what?"

"To find me."

Clare considered that for a moment; he realized how quickly Jing had responded to his outburst. Then he became very upset. "Don't tell me that you've been *following* me."

The man chuckled.

Clare closed his disbelieving eyes. "What?" he seethed. "I can't believe this." He shook his head. "This is insane. You," he added, pointing to the man, "must be *insane* to follow me up a river for two weeks."

"Oh," said the man, "it's all quite sane. You simply let go of your need to find me, and there I was. That's how the world works, you know."

Clare did not know what to say. He was irate. After a dense minute, he said, "And you're supposed to be a *teacher?* Who would trust someone like you to teach them?" He didn't wait for a response. "What do you teach, anyway?"

"Trust," the man replied with a flourishing bow.

Clare sat down. He was being mocked by a jester, in the middle of the wilderness. He was at a loss. Finally the man sat down next to him.

"I'll tell you what," Jing proposed, crossing his legs. "If you can sit here for half an hour, I have nothing to offer. If not," he continued, "then I will teach you how to sit."

Clare looked at him. "Teach me how to sit," he echoed weakly.

"Yes."

Clare covered his face with his hands.

"Shall we begin?" Jing asked cheerfully.

The boy raised his head. "You don't think I can *sit* here for a half-hour?"

"I'm not certain," admitted the man.

Clare sighed deeply. "Yes," he said wearily. "Let's begin."

Jing smiled and fixed his gaze on the rushing river. Clare frowned and crossed his legs like his companion's. The two sat in silence. While they were sitting, a bird passed by overhead. A nearly invisible fish negotiated a bit of white water in the stream below. The clouds parted to reveal the sun, and the hot day grew immediately hotter.

Sweat began to run from Clare's forehead. First it came over him like a damp shiver; then it gathered into droplets which rolled irreverently down his cheeks. He wiped the moisture away.

A family of gnats began to flirt with his mouth. He brushed them away with a slap, but they came back. Again he slapped at them, and then blew them away, but again they came back. One flew into his nose and stayed there.

Clare heaved a breath through his nostrils, wondering if the gnat was gone. He heaved another breath, and blew the cloud of gnats away again. Time passed, and the sweat dripped from his armpits, rolling down the sides of his chest.

Clare looked over at Jing, but the man remained unmoved. He blew the gnats away again. Just then a mosquito bit his knee. He slapped it, and flicked the smashed body away from him.

He noticed an ant moving in the grass near his foot. He thought about it for a moment. He also thought about the gnat that had flown into his nose. At that point, he felt something crawling on his leg, and flicked away a rather large spider. Another mosquito stung the back of his neck. He slapped it, and sweated some more.

Eventually the ant found its way into his undershorts. This, Clare decided, would be a challenge. He allowed it to crawl around for a while, and then he began to wonder. What if it wasn't an ant? An ant crawling around in one's undershorts is pretty bad, he decided, but what if it's something else? What if it's one of those worms with legs? What if it's one of those black beetles with pincers? What if it's one of those fat, dirty cockroaches he had seen in the city, crawling around in his undershorts? What if it's something worse than *that*? He tolerated the last thought for only an instant.

"*Ahhh!*" Clare shouted, ripping off his pants. He had been sitting for a minute and a half. He looked over at Jing, but the man remained serenely unmoved. Clare searched through his removed undershorts, but he found nothing. He frowned. "OK, fine," he said. "You win."

Jing showed not the slightest sign of response. Clare wandered around the area for the remainder of the half-hour, and then returned to the site. "Time's up," he announced. But the man continued to sit.

Clare went for a swim, fixed himself dinner, and decided to camp for the night. He fell asleep, woke up, and still the man sat by the river. It wasn't until a full twenty-four hours later that Jing finally turned his head. "I'm glad to see you're still here," he said.

By that time, Clare's disgust had turned to awe. "How in the world did you do that?" he asked.

"It's a matter of trust," the man explained, standing up.

"Trust?"

"One who trusts nature can do anything."

Clare thought of nature invading his undershorts. "You trust bugs?" he asked, obviously disappointed.

78

Jing smiled. "The bugs are part of nature, but nature goes far beyond what we can see. Nature is the flow of life."

"I don't understand," countered the boy.

Jing's face spread into a smile. "Ah," he said. "Now we can begin."

∽

The pair rose early the next morning. "Today we will sit," said Jing. "And that is all. Your time will move more fluidly, though. Today you will have a mantra."

"A mantra?" Clare asked.

Jing explained, "A mantra is a sound or idea upon which to center your thoughts. Yours is this: 'I need do nothing.' Repeat it to yourself. 'I need do nothing.'"

"I need do nothing," the attentive student replied.

Jing nodded. "Fill your mind with it. Let all other distractions float away. Focus your entire heart on the knowledge that you need do nothing."

A silence descended. "That's all?" Clare finally asked.

"That is all," Jing affirmed, positioning himself on the riverbank. "If you could realize the truth of this statement, you would find perfect freedom. Let's begin."

The man fixed his gaze on the rushing river. Clare respectfully crossed his legs like his companion's. The two sat in silence. A squirrel bounced through the leaves nearby. The wind whispered through the trees above. The morning sun climbed over a ridge, and the day became warm.

Sweat began to run from Clare's forehead. "I need do nothing. I need do nothing," he said to himself. He allowed the moisture to flow over his face. After a moment, a family of gnats began to play with his nose. "I need do nothing," he told them, allowing the congregation to buzz. An early-rising mosquito pierced his arm. He winced and allowed it to draw a luxurious amount of blood while he repeated the words, "I need do nothing." It flew away with loaded red sacs.

An ant crawled in the grass by his leg. "I need do nothing," he thought. It crawled into his pants. "I need do nothing," he thought. Sweat poured from his creased brow. "I need do nothing. I need do nothing."

Another ant crawled into his pants. He considered the possibility that he might be sitting on an anthill. Two more ants crawled into his pants, and still he chanted to himself, "I need do nothing." He could feel them exploring his undershorts. Another one crawled in, and one of the original entrants crawled up his chest. He shifted his weight, and one bit him. It hurt. "I need do nothing," he assured himself, trying to ignore the sting. "I need do nothing." Another one crawled in.

This continued for quite some time. By the thousandth-or-so repetition of his statement, hundreds of ants were crawling through Clare's clothes. He had been bitten several times, and was sure he was sitting on an anthill. "I need do nothing. I need do nothing," he continued, watching a rather large black ant creep down his nose. "I need do nothing." At long last the light came.

"Wait!" he screamed to his tranquil companion, making sure to remain unmoved in case he was wrong. "If I need do nothing, then I need not sit here! *Right?*"

"Of course not," Jing said with a merry laugh.

"Ahhh!" shouted Clare as he ripped away his clothes and dove into the river. The water plucked the ants from his hair, from his ears and underarms and toes. "Ahhh," he breathed with relief, splashing around a bit for good measure. When the boy was sufficiently cleansed, his naked body climbed the bank.

"Jing," he asked. "Why didn't you *tell* me that I didn't have to sit there?"

"What did I tell you?"

"That I need do nothing," Clare answered. He paused. "Oh." Another pause. "Well, then, why should I sit here at all?"

"Only because you may find it deeply peaceful," Jing replied. "That is all."

Clare decided that he'd rather do other things. He clomped around in the woods for a while and took a brief excursion upstream. At one point during the day, he found a sufficiently bug-free spot and sat for a few minutes. It wasn't as difficult as he had expected. At dinnertime, the boy retraced his path back to the man.

"Jing," he asked over a simple dinner, "why do you like to sit by the river? Why not in the forest, or somewhere else?"

His companion finished chewing a piece of bread. "The river is one of nature's greatest symbols. It reminds me of the way."

Clare thoughtfully stroked the stubble on his face. "You haven't exactly explained this 'nature' concept to me," he said.

"Nature," explained the man, spreading out his arms, "is the flow of life. It is an effortless flow, like the river. No struggle is necessary."

"And life is the same, you're saying?"

"Even more than we realize. Everything we need will come to us if we trust. Everything: food, shelter, companionship, security. Like the river, they will flow into our lives if we simply allow them to."

"You can't really believe that," decided Clare. "You can't really believe that no work is necessary."

"I can, and I do," said Jing. "As long as this 'work' of yours requires effort, it is unnecessary. And if it is effortless, then it's not truly work."

Clare shook his head. "No way."

"I won't argue with you," said Jing. "Because that would require effort." He grinned. "However, if you like, I will show you a symbol from my past. You were heading upstream anyway, am I correct?"

Clare nodded.

"Good. Tomorrow we shall walk." With that he returned to his sitting position and closed his eyes. Around him, the long day faded into night.

∾

They hiked for several days along the riverbank. Few words interfered with the sound of the rushing water. Just as Clare was beginning to worry about their dwindling food supplies, Jing abruptly stopped. "Here we are," he said.

The boy looked around. The area was relatively nondescript, except for a rather large depression in the earth. He dropped his bag and ambled over to it. The edges of the sloping hole contained some crumbled fragments of brick, but that was all. He raised his eyebrows to Jing.

"I once lived here," Jing told him. "Let's sit and eat, and I will tell you the story of a man who tried to fight nature." They took the last of Clare's provisions from his bag and began upon a modest lunch. "Many years ago I left my home," said Jing after finishing his portion. He wiped the crumbs from his mouth with a small pocket cloth. "I was filled with bold ambition, ready to tackle the world. I planned to become very rich and powerful." He stood, walked to the river, and drank from it with cupped hands. Returning to the seated boy, he continued. "I came to this spot armed with a detailed dream and a muscled crew. My plan was to conquer the river. I was to build the greatest dam with the greatest spinning waterwheel, and harness the energy of the flow. You can see what remains."

Clare cast his glance upon the rushing stream. It ran unchecked. "Did you build it?" he asked.

"Yes," replied Jing. "It took us nearly a year to fashion the wheel and secure the wooden dam, but we did it. It was magnificent—the product of an engineering genius. After it was complete, we built a giant factory. That hole," he said, pointing to the spot, "was once its foundation. We built machine upon machine, bristling with cogs and levers and staggering cams. We pumped out ten thousand units the first year and sold them throughout the land. The next year we produced fifty thousand. I managed the factory, oversaw the engineers, graphed the projections. The factory was me, and I was it."

"Was it fun?" inquired Clare during a pause. "Were you happy?"

"No," the man said. "I was anxious. Always very anxious. The years rushed by like the river—I kept building, investing, planning, and plotting, always striving to increase production. I thank nature for the great flood."

Clare raised his eyebrows. "What flood?"

"Twenty or so years after I dammed the river, a giant rainstorm came. The river overflowed its banks and drowned my machines. The waterwheel ripped loose from its fastenings. The factory crumbled. My laborers and I had to climb to higher ground; we couldn't prevent the breaking of the dam."

"What did you do?" asked a concerned Clare.

Jing paused for a moment. "When the storm was over, I sat down by the remains of my dam and prepared to die. My workers left; they knew that my life was over. I sat and watched the pieces of wood rip loose and float around the bend. Each splinter was like a knife in my side. When the last fragment finally broke free, I bowed my head. The end had come."

"But you didn't die," the boy pointed out.

"Indeed I did," insisted Jing with a slight smile. "I gave up my life. I had failed. But, as you note, I was reborn. Nature brought me a fish."

Clare looked puzzled.

"As I sat, dead in spirit and nearly starved, a fish jumped from the water onto the riverbank. It came to me. That fish truly saved my life—it brought hope to the hopeless."

"And so what did you do?"

"I did the only thing that I could—I ate the fish and continued to trust. Two more leaped from the stream that afternoon. Another came the following morning. I understand now that it was a normal spawning phenomenon, but at the time it was truly miraculous. Nature restored my life."

"Did the fish keep jumping?" asked the boy.

"No. But as I continued to trust, knowing that I had no other choice, I began to understand the true way of the world. I began to see things—honeycomb, fragrant nuts, animals prepared to offer their bodies. I didn't question the means by which nature provided. I simply accepted."

"And you stayed alive," Clare concluded.

"Better than that," returned Jing. "I began to truly live. Each day of my new life affirmed the lesson that I need do nothing. Each day of effortless existence increased my trust. In its wonderful certainty, my life became joyful."

Clare smiled at the story. After a minute he said, "So I suppose you can figure out what we're going to eat for dinner."

"Nature will," Jing said, walking over to the water's edge. He peered between the currents and eddies and asked, "Would you mind stepping out onto that rock?"

Clare took a leap. "This one?" he asked.

"Yes. Reach into the water on your left-hand side."

Clare did, and quickly pulled his hand out. "There's something there!" he exclaimed.

"Our dinner, I suspect," said Jing with a grin. "And a lesson."

∾

A few days later, the boy turned to his quiet teacher. "Jing," he asked with a trace of frustration, "do you have any other phrases besides 'I need do nothing'? I'm getting bored with it."

"One is all you need," said the man.

"Yeah, I know. But do you have any others, anyway?"

The man chuckled. "Try this: 'If I defend myself, I am attacked.' It holds the answer to everything you seek."

"If I defend myself, I am attacked." Clare thought about it. "Why's that?"

"Because," said Jing, "you build your defenses out of the only substance that can hurt you—fear."

"Wait," requested Clare, scratching his head. "I don't understand. What 'defenses' are these?"

"Samara sent you, correct?" asked Jing.

"Well, yes."

"Didn't she tell you her story of the swordsman?"

"Oh yeah," said Clare, remembering. "But I don't see what that has to do with defending myself against ants."

"You and your ants," Jing laughed to himself. "OK. Let's say that you're afraid of being bitten by an ant. Or say that you're afraid of being poor, or anything else. As soon as you begin to build defenses against that fear, you make it very real in your life. Pretty soon you're huddling in terror behind huge walls of fear."

"But at least you're not being bitten by ants."

"But you are; in your dreams and hidden fears, you're living the bite over and over again. It haunts you every moment. That's why some people are so anxious all the time—they're terrified of an imagined threat. And very few of them are willing to lower their defenses, even for an instant, to see if the ants are real or not." He looked closely at the boy. "Trust me. I've lived such a life."

"So are you saying that everyone needs to have their defenses ripped away like your dam?"

"No, I think not," said Jing. "That was the only

way I could have found freedom. You can lower yours gradually, though. Be gentle on yourself; nature certainly is."

"OK. But what am I supposed to do about the ants?"

"Just let go," said the man. "Just stop fighting. As I said, you need do nothing—you need not fight, or struggle, or suffer. Let the ants flow through your life. They won't attack you."

"If I defend myself, I am attacked," Clare returned with a nod. He turned back in a few minutes. "But Jing, can I brush them off if they climb on me?"

"Of course," smiled the man, keeping his eyes on the stream. "They'd probably rather have you do that anyway."

"Good," breathed Clare with relief.

∾

The young student practiced his lessons for weeks. While Jing seemed masterfully settled, Clare was forced to take his sitting periods in five-minute chunks. There was just too much noise in his head. The boy spent the rest of his time splashing in the stream or walking through the forest. He noticed that if he tried his best he could pass through the trees with only a ripple of sound. It was a wonderful game, trying to creep close to the chipmunks and birds, and he found the challenge much more interesting than sitting. One day he announced this to Jing.

"Well," said the man, "what seems to be your problem? Nothing could be easier than sitting in silence."

"I can't really sit for more than ten minutes," admitted Clare. "If the bugs don't get me, it's the noise in my head. There are just too many thoughts in there."

"It's easy if you let them flow," Jing said. "Don't fight them. Don't analyze them. Just let them be."

Clare sat down and really tried to let them flow, but they refused to. Instead, they seemed to accumulate and multiply until he had thousands of ideas buzzing around in his brain. He shook himself. "No. This isn't working," he told the man. "There's too much garbage in there. I'm going for a walk."

"Wait," said Jing. "This is the time for discipline. Let's begin."

Clare sat back down with a concerned look on his face.

"I want you to speak your thoughts out loud. I want you to give them a voice."

"Out loud?" asked Clare.

"Yes, out loud."

"But they're not really words. Some of them are pictures, or just feelings. It's kind of a mess in there."

"It's all right. It will come," the man reassured him. "Let's begin."

Clare waited for a minute. "Um, there's some blue in there," he said.

"Say it: 'blue.'"

"Blue," said the boy. "Blue . . . blue river . . . my mom . . . blue sky . . . clouds . . . Is this right?"

"Yes. It's fine," said Jing. "But free yourself up. Shout if you want, or sing. You can have a *blue* or a bluuee or a blaaaa. Let go." He nodded supportively.

"OK. Forest . . . river . . . river . . . fish . . . oooooowaaaaaa . . . river . . . sitting . . . dumb sitting . . . the river won't get out of there . . . there's . . . a river . . . in my head . . . bluuee riiiver . . . "

"How do you feel right now?" asked Jing.

". . . hiking . . . kind of annoyed, I guess . . . river river river . . . "

"Let the anger come out, then. Give it a voice."

". . . dumb, dumb river . . . I *hate* this . . . I hate sitting here . . . I'm hungry . . . what are we going to have for dinner . . . *river river* . . . I hate this . . . "

"Who's speaking right now?" asked Jing.

". . . I hate rivers . . . I am . . . riverriver . . . I am speaking, and this is no fun . . . "

Quickly Jing asked, "But is it your joy that is speaking? Or your excitement? Or your anger? Or your fear?"

". . . riva riva riva . . . my anger . . . this is my anger . . . anger . . . anger . . . river . . . flowin' on . . . anger . . . anger . . . I hate this . . . I hate sitting here . . . "

"Say it: 'I am anger.' Repeat it."

". . . riv . . . I am anger . . . I am anger . . . Like this? I am anger . . . I am anger . . . "

"Yes. And how do you feel?"

". . . angry . . . I am anger, and I am angry . . . I am anger, and I am angry . . . I am anger, and I am angry."

"Keep going. Louder."

"*I am anger and I am angry . . . I am anger and I am angry . . . I am anger and I am angry! I am anger and I am . . .* "

"Who are you?" asked Jing.

Clare's body shook with his words. ". . . *afraid . . . I am anger and I am afraid! I am anger and I am afraid! I am . . . fear and I am afraid! I am fear and I am afraid!* I am . . . " At this point, the boy's voice dissolved into a quake of sobs. The old man cradled him in his arms and absorbed a reservoir of tears. "I'm really afraid of this," came a small, trembling voice after a while. "It's so scary."

"I know," said Jing. "It's the scariest thing in the world."

Clare lifted his head. "But why?" he asked, wiping his eyes with the back of his hand.

Jing smiled softly and shook his head. He rotated so that he was facing the boy. "We all have two voices running through our minds," he said. "One is a voice of fear; the other is a voice of peace. The voice of fear is a scary thing. But as we calmly listen to it, we begin to hear what it conceals—the beautiful voice of peace."

"Well, I have lots of voices in there," whispered Clare.

"No," smiled Jing. "It may seem like that, but it always comes down to those two. However, the voice of fear often speaks first and loudest. It spins a web of confusion to cover the other."

Clare sat for a moment. "So what can we do about it? Can't we just cut through it or something?"

"Indeed we can," said the man. "As you just did. It's scary, because it involves looking at fear itself. But for the moment, you've moved beyond it. You've lowered your defenses. Let's sit in silence for a few minutes."

Clare nodded. Forty-five minutes later, he opened his eyes with a smile.

∽

The boy spent several weeks with his teacher, practicing the process of trust. It was trust, he saw, that enabled him to break through the wall of fear. It was trust that led him beyond the voices of confusion. When Jing saw that the day had come, he informed his pupil.

"I suspect that it's time for you to move on," he said.

"I think you are right," returned Clare. "I still need to find my father." His voice carried a tone of maturity; his words now dropped with weight from his lips. The time he had spent with Jing had been filled with silence and knowing smiles, accompanied by an occasional inquiry into nature's design.

Daily he had broken through the voice of his fear. At first the exercise had progressed with a burst of tears, but by now there was only a confident stillness. He had finally arrived. His life was free of its confusion, and his mind was at peace. "I would be happy to stay a little while longer, however," he said with a bow.

Jing smiled. "A generous compliment from one who came in doubt."

Clare smiled back. "A compliment well deserved."

The old man stood. "Let's walk toward the mountains today. I have a friend you should meet."

"Is he also a teacher?"

"My friend is a true master," Jing said. "His name is Baba."

"A master?" asked Clare. "I can't imagine someone who you'd call 'master.'"

"You will be surprised," chuckled Jing. "Let us walk."

"Once I understood the way of nature," explained Jing as they strolled upstream, "everything became clear. I suddenly found that order was everywhere."

Clare thought back on his journey. "You must not have been to the city lately," he said.

Jing laughed. "Nature flows perfectly well through the city. It just takes an open mind to see it."

"A *very* open mind, perhaps."

"Yes, perhaps. But anyone who trusts nature will find it."

"You're probably right," said Clare, "but it's one thing to sit by a river. It's another thing to have a job or a bunch of responsibilities. I mean, you can't just trust that every meal will pop out at you if you live in the city."

"No?" asked Jing.

"Well, no. In the city you have to work for a living." He nodded to the river. "Fish don't hop out of the water there."

"Anyone can trust nature," said the man. "At any time, in any place."

"Do you really think so?" asked Clare. "Even someone with a job?"

"Certainly. And you can tell me how."

The boy looked surprised. "What do you mean?"

"Let's call it your final examination," the man winked. "Tell me how someone can perform a job without effort."

"Well, like who?"

"Let's take an artist, for example. How would an artist who trusts nature spend her day? How would she paint?"

Clare thought about the question for a while. "Well," he began, "she probably wouldn't worry too much about how her paintings turned out."

Jing nodded. "Probably. But how would she start? How would she choose something to paint?"

Clare thought to himself. "I guess *she* wouldn't do the choosing," he said. "She'd just wait until an image popped out at her."

"Indeed. And then what?"

Clare closed his eyes. "She'd wait until her creativity flowed through her. She wouldn't even *try* to do the painting by herself. She'd just wait for it to happen."

"Good," said Jing. "I think you're right. Now how about a teacher?"

"What kind of teacher?"

"Any kind," said Jing.

The boy thought about it. "A teacher who trusts nature? I guess if he trusted nature, he wouldn't worry about what to say. He wouldn't even think about his lessons. He'd just try to speak the truth—and the right words would pop out of his mouth. Is that right?"

"It sounds good to me. Now how about a factory owner?" asked Jing with a sly smile.

Clare laughed. He was feeling pretty confident now. "A factory owner who trusts nature will ride the ups and downs of his business like a kid on a roller coaster. He'll have fun. And by trusting nature, he'll remain aware of everything that needs to be done." Clare grinned. "He'll even know what to do in a flood."

"Ah!" cried Jing, clapping his hands together. "Wonderful! You have truly seen the way."

Clare smiled proudly.

"I have only one more question for someone of your knowledge. If life is like a river, please tell me—where does true happiness lie?"

The young man walked in silence for several minutes. Finally he said, "In the center of the flow."

"No," said Jing.

"No?" asked Clare with a frown.

"Perhaps one travels quickest in the center, but that isn't the answer. The answer is the ocean, where the waters are joined."

The boy was confused. "Wait. I don't understand. There's no flow in the ocean. Nature can't *be* there."

Jing laughed. "The ocean is the source of nature; the rivers are but pathways home." He asked another question. "Can you tell me why we study the rivers at all?"

"Why?" echoed Clare, clearly disconcerted. "Well, it seems kind of obvious." He felt his knowledge beginning to crumble.

"In order to let go," said the man definitively. "Letting go is our true function here."

"Letting go? Of what?" Clare was feeling quite unsure of himself at this point.

Jing waved his hands at the sky. "Our only task is to let go of our concepts, our beliefs, our ideas about the world. Trust, letting go—it's the same thing. We let go of the world, and we find ourselves home."

"But—" said Clare weakly. "I don't know if I understand."

"Well," said the chuckling Jing, placing his hand on the boy's shoulder. "Perhaps now you can continue your journey."

FOUR

"Know that you know nothing," were Jing's final words. "It will make your way clear." Clare was now bothered. All his newly acquired knowledge was laid bare by the man's merry laugh. Letting go of the world? He didn't exactly see where that fit in.

Well, he finally decided, Baba would certainly make everything clear. Baba the master! A master! Only the greatest would earn such a title from Jing.

For days, the eager traveler wrestled his way over boulders and up slippery talus slopes. Pebbles rolled beneath his feet and spilled down the path behind him. The way into the mountains proved to be tough and incessantly uphill.

He walked for days; after a while, everything dropped away except the goal. Jing and Samara became tiny wisps of memory. His home, his journey, even his father faded from his mind. Nothing mattered but the mountains. Baba, he had been told, lived in a palace at the top of the world. It would be a long trip.

Clare was completely out of breath when he reached the top of the first peak. At the moment, just slightly above him, an angry gray storm was preparing to strike. Clare rushed down the mountain's far side in his concern; he never even noticed the view. And thus the pace of his trip was set.

For weeks he trudged up and down in silence. Fog swirled around him; rain pelted down on him; mountain after mountain passed beneath his feet. He trailed sweat in the valleys and tiny cotton clouds of breath at the heights. But not once did he pause to take in the sights.

Several weeks into his silent climb, Clare was unexpectedly hit by a blast of cold wind. He shook his head awake. "Well hello, North Wind," he said with a smile. "I guess I've made it all the way to your home."

The North Wind spoke in tough, frigid blasts; all it said now was, "Wake up! Wake up!" Clare could never get much else out of the wind. His mother, though, had once heard it tell a tale.

"The lands to the north are very cold," she had explained to him. "And that is where the North Wind blows.

"One bright day," she continued, "the North Wind saw something strange: there below it, on the open land, was a farmer locked up in chains. The farmer was being led in the direction of the king's castle by three big soldiers. The North Wind swirled around the party for a few moments in order to hear their story."

And here is what the North Wind heard:

"I don't understand. I really don't understand."

This came from the poor farmer, who wept tears of bewilderment as he spoke. "I don't understand what I've done wrong. I'm just a poor farmer who works on the land. I've never done anything wrong."

One of the soldiers offered a suggestion. "Perhaps treason? Did you speak badly of the king?"

"No!" protested the farmer, shaking his head vigorously. "I love the king as much as anyone else."

"How about poaching?" asked another guard. "Have you killed any of the king's deer?"

"He probably refused to pay his taxes," interrupted the third.

"No! No!" cried the farmer. "I am a good citizen. I respect the king's property, and I pay my taxes as best I can." He hung his head as he spoke. "I've never done anything wrong in my life. And now I am a prisoner."

As the group marched toward the castle, the North Wind continued to hear their guesses. "Theft?" "Drunkenness?" "Forgot to honor the king's birthday?"

"No! No! No!" came the fading cries.

The wind rushed on to attend to other business that afternoon, but at the end of the day it crept back to investigate the man's fate. It easily found an entrance into the king's drafty castle and whipped its way through the rooms. Finally, in a stone cell at the top of a tower, it found the poor farmer.

The man was alone. The heavy wooden door that closed off his cell was locked. The wind seeped under a crack by the floor, and remained in the room to watch.

Eventually there came a knock on the door.

"Hello?" called the farmer hopefully. "Yes—hello? Please come in, whoever you are."

He heard some mumbling and a clatter of keys. Then the door opened to reveal a well-dressed servant. "Welcome," said the servant, bowing low. "It is our honor to accept your visit."

"Visit?" cried the farmer. "But I was locked up and brought here by a group of soldiers! I thought I was a *prisoner!*"

The servant looked confused. "A prisoner?" he said. "No, sir. Absolutely not. We have received orders from the king that you are to be a guest of honor at the castle tonight. Perhaps the guards misunderstood." He then bowed again. "I deeply apologize for any mistreatment."

The farmer let out a huge laugh of relief. Then he took one or two deep breaths to calm himself. "Well," he said. "Well, thank you. I must say, I *was* quite worried there. But this changes everything. Please tell the king that I look forward to meeting him. To tell you the truth, I've never even *seen* him before."

"Certainly," said the servant. "I will be back in a minute or two with a bowl of warm water for your bath. Please make yourself comfortable while I'm gone." He then glanced around the room. "Castle life isn't all that comfortable, but this is one of our finest quarters. I hope you'll find it to your liking."

The farmer nodded. When the servant was gone, he cast a fresh look over his room. It *was* rather nice, he admitted. The furniture was soft, and he had a nice view from the window. How funny to imagine himself a prisoner! He made himself comfortable in one of the chairs.

As he sat there, enjoying the idea of a meeting with the king, he heard another rattle at his door. This time a burly man burst into the room. "Unlocked?" the man bellowed at him. "Why is this unlocked?"

The farmer gripped the arms of his chair. "May I help you?" he asked meekly.

"Help me?" shouted the man, pointing a finger. "It seems like *you're* the one who needs help here. Who unlocked this door?"

"It was a servant," explained the anxious farmer. "He told me that I was a guest of honor for the king."

The guard erupted with laughter. "What a joke! It was probably that foolish page—he's always playing tricks on the prisoners." Then he said scoffingly,

"You'll be the guest of honor, all right. The guest for the king's executioner!" With a mighty bang, he slammed the door and locked it tight. The farmer listened to his laughter echo down the stone hallways.

Now the poor man dropped his head into his hands. "What cruel tricks my life plays!" he moaned. "It's true, just as I feared! I am to lose my head for no apparent reason." And he wept once again.

After a while the door opened. In walked the servant with a bowl of warm water. "You!" shouted the farmer, leaping to his feet. "You've tricked me! You told me that I was the king's guest of honor! Now I know that I am really a prisoner."

The servant was visibly shocked. "Why would you believe that?" he asked, laying the bowl at the farmer's feet.

"That man!" wailed the farmer. "The big one with the keys—*he* told me who you were. It is a cruel game that you play, toying with the minds of prisoners."

"My dear sir," said the servant, "I assure you that you are not a prisoner. Perhaps there is a misunderstanding among the guards, but that will be cleared up soon. You see, the king has assembled his whole court to meet you. It is a rare honor to be treated this way."

The farmer was now almost overwhelmed with confusion. "I'm not going to die tonight? You're certain the king wishes to welcome me?"

"Come with me," said the servant, motioning to the open door. "We shall ask the king himself."

The farmer walked through the castle halls with the servant. Several times he considered running away—or jumping out of a window—but he couldn't decide whether that would be appropriate. What if he *wasn't* a prisoner? What if the king really *did* wish to honor him?

Soon the farmer and the servant came to the king's throne room. The carpet that ran through the center of the hall was lined with rows of courtiers. Shields hung from the walls. The farmer walked slowly up to the man on the tall golden chair. Then he threw himself to his knees.

"Your Majesty," he wept humbly, "have mercy. I am just a poor farmer. I was brought here this afternoon, bound up in chains. First I was told that I was a guest of honor. Then I was told that I was a prisoner. Finally I was told that I was your guest again. Your Majesty, what have I done? Why am I here, and what is to become of me?"

The king smiled down on the poor farmer. Then he began to chuckle. And as he began to laugh more loudly, all the guards and courtiers in the room joined in with their own laughter.

"My poor farmer," said the king between breaths, "we do apologize." He chuckled to himself some more. "You see, every year, we choose a poor soul like yourself. We lock you up in chains, bring you to the castle, and reverse your fortune a few times. It's all such fun to watch. Anyway, you've been a good sport. We'll give you something for your troubles and send you back to your farm."

The farmer, who was crouched down anyway, now collapsed in relief upon the floor. When he was able to rise, he stood and mustered a smile. "Your Majesty," he said with some pride, "I suppose that even a poor farmer like me can laugh at himself. It *is* quite a funny joke you've played. Especially now that it's over."

"Well said!" said the king. "Treasurer!" he then called. "Count out twenty pieces of gold for this poor farmer who can laugh at himself."

As the treasurer was counting the money, a young boy quietly walked into the throne room. "Your Majesty!" cried the king unexpectedly, leaping from the chair. "We thought you had gone riding today." The king then kneeled before the boy.

"Jester," said the obviously irritated boy, smacking the head of the former king, "I warned you never again to sit on my chair. And you," he waved at the guards and courtiers, "how could you play along with this? I should throw you all out." The group bowed their heads in embarrassment.

Now the farmer was overcome with confusion. "Your Majesty?" he asked the boy.

"Yes," said the lad tersely. "Who are you? No— don't answer. I'll find out myself. Guard!"

A man strode humbly to the boy, offering a stack of written papers. "Here you are, sire," he said.

"All right," said the boy, settling down into the throne. "Let's see . . . " He read the first note and then he glanced at the farmer. "Oho!" he exclaimed. "The brother of that hated King Smire, are you? We've been trying to get ahold of you for a while."

"No!" cried the farmer, clutching desperately at his hair. "Your Majesty, I am but a poor farmer who has been plucked from his land. I am your loyal subject now, as I have always been."

"Look here," snapped the young king, leaning forward. "If the paper says you're Smire's brother, then you are. Execute him!"

A guard approached the farmer and attached a pair of shackles to his arms. But then the king called out again: "Wait, you fool!" He leafed through the papers. "Guard, you brought me *last* week's papers. We've already done away with Smire's brother. Unlock this fellow." He tossed the stack of papers back into the guard's face. "So who *are* you?" he asked the poor farmer.

The farmer was trembling. The strain of this day was too much to bear. "I am a farmer," he said.

The king's face clouded. "That's it? You're just a farmer? You work on my land?"

"Yes, My Lord," said the farmer, beginning to breathe easier. "Your Majesty, I am your humble and loyal servant. That is all."

"Is this true?" he asked his chief guard.

"Yes, sire," replied the man, stepping up. "We brought him here this afternoon."

The young king leaned back in his chair. He looked down at the trembling man. "I suppose that we brought you here by mistake," he observed.

The farmer gave a weak laugh. "Well, Your Majesty, that's quite all right. I suppose that mistakes *do* happen from time to time."

The king thought for a while. Then he turned to his guard. "Kill him anyway," he said. "He's been too much trouble."

The guards rushed over and the farmer collapsed once again. As they were attaching a pair of metal cuffs to his ankles, a tall woman walked into the room.

"My young duke," she said calmly to the boy on the throne, instantly stilling all activity in the room, "I think that you have not yet proven yourself worthy of that chair. Leave kingly games for the king."

The boy frowned and crossed his arms. "I'll have the throne soon enough," he sneered at her. Then he stood and strode out of the room.

The woman now turned to the poor farmer. "Welcome, sir," she said. "May I ask why you are here?"

At this point the farmer simply gave up. He knew that he could no longer endure the day's cycles. For a while he sat on the ground, thinking. Then he raised his head and said, "Madam, I truly do not know. Once I was a poor farmer. Now my life is in your hands."

The woman looked at him curiously. "You were a poor farmer?" she asked. He nodded. "And now you place your life in my hands?" He nodded again.

"Then," she announced with a surprised laugh, "I suppose we shall have to make you our king!" She explained: "You see, for many years our kingdom has been without a ruler—we've tried to keep it a secret. We have been waiting patiently for the right person to arrive, but no one until today has appeared.

"Before the old king died," she continued, "he left us with a prophecy. He said, 'The person who will succeed me will be a poor and simple man who has loosed his grasp on the world.' You seem to be the one."

The farmer blinked his eyes. "Truly, My Lady," he replied, rising to meet her, "nothing would surprise me now." He then followed her to the great royal chair and took his seat upon it. Slowly he shook his head.

"Today," said the man, "my fortune has turned from good to bad like a spinning coin. The game has worn me out. But at last," he said, "perhaps I see the answer: *true* fortune comes when we put that spinning coin to rest."

And from then on, the farmer ruled over the land as a wise and much-loved king.

Clare's mother rubbed her son's head after the story. "Do you know what the North Wind said after that?"

"What?"

"It said, 'That farmer is now the happiest man I know. Every day is like a gift to him.'"

"Did the wind say anything else?" the boy wanted to know.

His mother thought. "No, I think that's all it said. But the North Wind learned quite a lesson from that farmer."

The boy looked surprised. "The winds can learn lessons from people?"

"Sure," said the woman. "The winds learn. And then they teach other people what they've learned."

"Well, what did the North Wind learn?"

"The North Wind learned that it's OK to give up."

The boy unexpectedly rolled up his sleeves and flexed his arm muscles for her. "I don't ever give up," he said.

"No?"

"Nope. I'm too strong for that."

"Well," said the woman, patting his behind, "just remember what happened when the farmer gave up. It's really the only way to become a king."

❧

Clare thought about the conversation as he wove

his way up the mountainside. Maybe that's what Jing was hinting at—trust, giving up, letting go of the world. Isn't that what the farmer did? Isn't that how he became king? He decided to think about it some more later.

For now he fastened his coat against the cold North Wind and redoubled the pace of his step. Patches of snow dotted the path; up this high, even in summer, the air was fairly chill.

Clare walked and walked, wondering about Baba's palace. Finally he came in sight of the goal. Here was the land's most majestic mountain, capped by a distant summit lodge. Baba's home, he supposed. With an enthusiastic groan, the young man pushed forward.

And a few days later he arrived. Before him, stretching far into the heavens, was the palace he'd dreamed of. It was an impossibly huge sight, decked with golden spires and marble arches. Clare was dazzled. He trembled as he entered its great double doors.

One hundred and six carefully counted steps he took down a long corridor, the noise of his boots echoing throughout the empty galleries. His last step took him into a towering atrium where an old, bearded man sat alone on a chair. "Master," offered Clare as he kneeled and dropped his head to the floor.

A few seconds passed as he bowed. There was a brief sound of shuffling; then there was only silence. As Clare continued to kneel upon the ground, he began to wonder what to do.

How did one act before a master? he wondered. Was it proper to raise one's head? No, he decided—that might be considered impolite. He resolved to wait until Baba commanded him to rise or something.

A few minutes passed. Clare began to feel awkward, kneeling with a bowed head in the middle of the huge room. Was he doing something wrong? Why didn't the master *say* something? He frowned and drove his eyes through the floor.

Many more minutes passed. By this point, Clare was sure that he was doing something wrong. His face burned with embarrassment; yet, he was loath to raise his head. What if by raising his head he offended the great Baba? A year of kneeling in silence upon the floor would be preferable to that. He continued to rest upon his now-throbbing knees.

Finally, at some point that afternoon, an exasperated Clare lifted his eyes. To his surprise, he found the great master kneeling in a similar fashion twenty steps before him. Clare studied the man's back for a few moments. Then he whispered loudly, "Sir?"

Baba turned his head. The man's face was richly colored, and his eyes danced along with a swaying white beard. "Yes?" he hissed back.

"Sir," Clare asked carefully. "Who are you bowing to?"

Baba replied, "Why, the master, of course!" He spoke in a hushed voice. "You must have seen him behind my chair. Is he still there?"

Clare shifted uncomfortably on his sore knees. "Sir," he explained, "I was bowing to you."

At this, the aged man sprung to his feet, spun around with a spirited agility, and shouted, "Me? Why in the world would you do *that*?"

Clare decided that he'd better remain kneeling just in case. "Well, sir," he began. "I was told that you are a true master." He tipped his head forward. "You are, aren't you?"

Baba laughed loudly, moving toward the prostrated boy. "My young friend, there is only one master. And he doesn't sit on chairs like this." He offered a hand. "Now, please get up. There are easier ways to bow."

Clare slowly stood, his joints crackling loudly. "Well then," he asked, shaking the kinks from his knees. "If you're not a master, who are you?"

"I am but a student. And a teacher, like you."

Clare started abruptly. "Sir, I assure you that I am no teacher." He considered himself. "I guess that you could say I'm a traveler who finally made it to the top of the mountain, but that's all."

"If you're not a teacher," said the man, "then you are the only one."

"Sir?"

"My friend," called Baba over his shoulder, diving behind the great chair to pull out two hidden cushions and a pot of steaming tea. "What I'm trying to say is that we're *all* teachers. Some of us just have a good time doing it." He slapped the cushions on the floor, and motioned for the boy to sit. Clare accepted, wondering where the teapot came from. "You must have spent time with Jing," said Baba, interrupting his thoughts.

"Yes," said Clare, looking up. "He helped me to see the way."

"Of course," laughed Baba, offering the young man an artfully crafted cup. "What else can one do?"

Clare turned the cup to examine the orange liquid inside. He took a sip. "This is wonderful," he said with a nod toward the tea. "But sir, where did it come from?"

"From infinite abundance!" cried the man, out-stretching his arms. "Where else?" Clare didn't have an answer for that one; he drank his share in silence. "I trust that your journey into the mountains was drenched with beauty," said Baba after a minute.

Clare thought back upon the last few foggy weeks. "Well, it was actually pretty tough. It rained a lot, I think."

Baba pointed a finger at him. "If the way was tough," he said, "then you *must* have gone the wrong way." He returned his teacup to the tray. "Only the path of joy leads anywhere."

Clare rubbed his knees. "Sir, my path was set long ago."

"By whom?"

"Well, by me. I'm looking for my father, and I fig-ured that the view from the highest mountain might give me some direction."

"But your journey hasn't been filled with joy?"

"Well, no, not *filled*. But I guess I have learned a lot."

"And this is what you've climbed all that way for?" Baba asked. "This is it?"

Clare smiled, and took a deep breath. "Yes," he said, looking around. "Yes. I suppose so."

"Depressing!" shouted the man, clutching the top of his head with his hands. "This is it?" He stood, and swept around the vaulted room. "This is what you've hiked all that way for?" He waved his arms around. "This? It can't be!" Clare was quite taken aback. "Now, follow me," continued the dancing Baba. "I'll show you what you really came for." He darted off toward a spiral staircase standing in an unnoticed corner of the room.

Clare groaned at the sight of stairs, but obediently rose and coaxed his stiff legs forward. Mounting the staircase, the pair climbed up and around and around. When Clare knew that he could not possibly lift another leg, the stairs yielded to an uncovered turret. "The top," announced Baba without a trace of exertion. "And your answer: the sky."

They emerged onto an open platform that supported two strange-looking chairs. The view of the mountains was utterly magnificent, and Clare was transfixed. This indeed was his answer—the view from the top of the world. The bumpy land flowed away in every direction, reaching its end at a perfectly unbroken, circular horizon. The boy spun around, shaking his head in awe. It was worth it all.

"Ahem," said Baba, and then with a flourishing upward motion, "the sky!"

Clare looked at the man, and then raised his eyes to the bowl of blue. It was certainly beautiful. Perfectly blue, perfectly round. Then he lowered his eyes to the wondrous mountain range and smiled again.

Baba frowned. "Let's sit," he said. He then leapt into one of the chairs, which pivoted backward into a near-horizontal recline. Clare lowered himself into the other and tipped backward in a similar fashion. From this vantage, there was only the sky. An endless, soothing wash of blue filled his eyes.

"Yes," he concurred. "This is nice."

"This," said Baba, "is your answer."

"Why do you keep saying that?" asked Clare. "It's only the sky."

"The sky is the infinite," replied Baba. "And there is nothing greater in this world."

"Nothing greater than the sky?" He thought that the mountains, at least, were more interesting.

"Nothing. Let me share a story with you."

Clare settled into his seat.

"I have only a few memories of my childhood," began the old man. "Little snatches float by, here and there. To begin with, I was raised in an orphanage, where they didn't feed us very well. The food they served was gray and mushy—not exactly the kind of thing to warm a little boy's heart, you know. I spent most of my time wandering about, dreaming of the day when I would have all the tastes my poor belly craved: things like roasted chickens and rolls and gravy and blueberry pies. Every couple of days I pressed my face against the grocer's window, just to remind myself that food came in different colors.

"There was a bakery in the neighborhood, too, and once a week I would crawl into it on my belly. The pastry rack reached almost to the floor, and I found I could sneak in, steal whatever was on the lowest shelf, and squirm my way back out the door without the baker seeing me. Those old muffins I stole gave me hope." He smiled. "They made my life a little bit sweet.

"Anyway," he continued, "there came a time when I just couldn't take the gray stuff anymore. I needed something better. My belly was grumbling louder than thunder, and I decided to break my only rule—I visited the bakery two days in a row." He turned to face Clare, propping himself up in his chair. "I knew that it was a bad idea. I knew what could happen, but I was a desperate little fellow.

"I crawled into the bakery as usual that day. And I nearly cried when I saw that the low shelves were empty. But then, as I slid back toward the door, I almost cried out again—this time for joy. For there on the floor was a strawberry tart!"

Baba smiled as he recalled the shape. "Oh, it was huge to my eyes, spilling over with whipped cream. I think it even had a bit of cocoa on top. I slowly reached for my prize, and then—very slowly, as if in a dream—it began to float away. How awful it was! I gave a cry, made a desperate grab, and was immediately collared by the big powdered baker. His clever trap had caught a clever mouse. The baker picked me up into the air and stared at me with the biggest eyes I'd ever seen.

"Oh, those eyes!" said Baba, remembering. "I, of course, began to cry. The baker kept holding me, looking more and more confused at my tears. Then he clutched my little body to his chest. I think he suddenly saw how similar we were. He threw off his apron, marched down to the orphanage, and adopted me as his son. That's how I found a new home."

Clare asked him, "Did your life change a lot? With your new father?"

"Immensely," said Baba. "I was in heaven. Everything I had dreamed about was now in my reach: the pastries, the tarts, the mountains of cookies. My father was kind; he let me eat whatever I wanted. I spent almost every day in the bakery, working side by side with him. It was quite perfect," smiled Baba, "until my hunger began to fade.

"You see, one day—I must have been about your age—I came into the shop and simply wasn't hungry. In fact, I was bored. There was nothing to eat that I hadn't tried fifty times. I knew the tastes, the textures—even the recipes—for every single sweet. By that time in my life, the memories of the orphanage had faded away. Without them, the bakery seemed to lose its magic."

"So what did you do?" asked Clare. "Did you leave home?"

"I became quite discouraged," said Baba. "Everything I had ever dreamed of was mine, and I wasn't content. Work at the bakery soon became monotonous—I could barely stand the sight of pies. Between the endless hours spent rolling dough, I began to work on another dream. I decided to create the most fabulous dessert in the world. I dreamed that it would sell far and wide, that it would make me rich and famous. The dream brought energy back to my life.

"I began working with a passion, searching for the best ingredients: nutmeg from the islands, vanilla from the jungles, sweet coconut cream from paradise itself. I worked day and night. I guarded my ideas. I hovered over my concoctions like a sorcerer steeping his brew.

"For years I slaved, pushing my limits, until finally I had what I wanted. 'The Last Temptation' I called it, and—oh! it sold well. Everyone wanted a taste. Through contracts and orders, I leveraged the idea into a mass of wealth. I was a very rich man by the time it fell out of style.

"At that point," continued Baba, "I began to spend. The funny thing was that my fortune kept growing. I bought jewels and resold them for five times their original price. I bought pounds and pounds of rare delicacies, ate my fill, and sold the rest at a profit. It was an exciting life—better than I had ever imagined. Anything was mine for a wish."

"But," interrupted Clare, "were you happy?"

"Oh, yes," replied Baba. "It was a wonderful life, filled with freedom and delight. Except," he added, "it didn't last. Like the wonders of the bakery, the wonders of my wealth enticed me only so long as they were new. Once I had retired my father to a life of luxury, once the bakery was sold and my memories of it distant, my new life became slow. And then tiresome.

"I began clutching at straws—doubling my consumption rate, tripling it. I embarked on endless vacations, hired more servants, sponsored great banquets. But nothing worked. Like before, the magic was gone. My disillusionment grew, and I withdrew into a private world of despair.

"I lived like that for years. And then, one day, a woman burst into my chambers—I don't know how she got past the guards—and spat on the floor before me. 'You hoard your money while others starve,' she said. 'You don't deserve to live like this.' I stirred, as if awakening from a dream.

" 'What would you have me do?' I asked her.

" 'Share what you have, this wealth,' she said, waving at a chandelier. 'Share it with the orphans, the poor. They certainly need it more than you do.'

"Right then and there, I saw the answer. With the woman watching, I reached for a cane and knocked my chandelier from the ceiling. I plucked off the jewels and gave them to her. And thus I began my life as a benefactor.

"This new life was far more exciting than any other I'd experienced. I hired ten cooks for my old orphanage (two of them pastry chefs), threw heaps of money at the parish houses, and nobly offered vagrants the clothes from my back. I paved the streets with my gold, and it felt glorious. I felt free. Strangers offered me their hands with tears of gratitude. Babies smiled at me. It would have been truly perfect, except for one thing."

"It didn't last?" guessed Clare.

"Exactly. And that was the saddest thing of all. You see, the whole thing felt like a game. And when the game became boring I began to worry—for this was clearly my last chance in the world. I continued on for a while, too terrified to admit that real happiness might be impossible." He paused, drawing a deep breath. "Finally, when I could deceive myself no longer, I broke down. It was over. In utter depression, I gave up on my life. I spent a fortune building this palace—this tomb—to carry me to my grave. The rest of my money I gave away."

"So what happened?" asked Clare. "Did you finally find happiness when you got to the top of the mountain?"

"No," said Baba. "I spent several years in the shadows of this cold and lonely building without a trace of hope. It's a wonder that I stayed alive. As I saw it, the view from the top of the world was unbearably sad. And I was at the top."

"Well, what happened?" demanded Clare. He pivoted around to confront the man. "You must have found *something*."

"I found the sky," said Baba. "Finally."

"What does that mean?"

Baba smiled. "I finally found an answer not of this world, an answer which showed me the infinite. One day I climbed to this roof and lay upon my back. I stayed on the spot for twenty days. Through sunny days and shooting stars, I just stared at the sky. It was so simple, so beautiful. On the twentieth day, a light exploded in my mind—the light of limitlessness, I guess you could say. In that instant I found my answer."

"Just by staring at the sky?"

"Perhaps I was ready. Goodness knows I had tried everything else. In that instant, everything moved into focus. I understood why my past had been filled with shifting pleasures: it's simply the nature of the world. I saw that true happiness must lie beyond. I saw that only the infinite will satisfy any of us."

"The infinite *what?*" Clare asked.

"The infinite peace. The infinite joy. Or perhaps more precisely, the experience of infinite *being*. No amount of pastries or possessions or donations can contain it. And nothing else will satisfy us."

Clare settled back into his seat. "You learned that, just by looking at the sky?"

"I had been learning it for a while. My father helped me to see, as did all my mistakes. In truth, I can't believe I had been ignorant for so long. Life in a world of limits seems immeasurably sad."

The two sat in silence for a while, focusing on the endless depths.

"You know," said Baba, "we all must surrender to it eventually."

But by that time, Clare was fast asleep.

∾

When he awoke, the sky was a blaze of blue. The western horizon shimmered icy-white; the east was the color of midnight. In between were a countless variety of other shades. The whole thing was so beautiful and perfectly simple that Clare again closed his eyes. When he reopened them he found that Baba was still sitting next to him.

"I do indeed bow to this," Clare said quietly, shivering a bit in the cool mountain air.

Baba smiled. "And the sky is always there for us. Come on," he added, "let's go eat." Rising from his spot, Baba offered his companion a supportive hand. Clare's legs were hopelessly cramped, and it took a mighty effort to leave the comfort of his chair.

They wound their way down the staircase, through the throne room, and into a narrow corridor. When at last they came before a set of large double doors, Clare expected to enter a kitchen. Instead, Baba flung wide the portal to reveal a giant dining hall.

Clare's breath flew from his body. In the center of the room was a huge, overflowing table. Here was a champagne fountain; there was a sculpted paté. A sparkling chandelier presided over the display, showering the room in dazzling light.

On the table, twenty places had been marked off with polished silver and folded white napkins. Before Clare could sputter a shocked demurral, Baba strode into the room and pulled out the head chair for his guest.

"Please," he said with a motion of his hand when he noticed that Clare still stood by the doorway.

"But," said the boy, "this is—well, so *extravagant*." He took a few steps forward, spinning his head to take in the sight. He then gave Baba a pointed look. "I thought you gave away all your money."

"Ah, yes," said Baba with a little cough. "The money. Well, I did *give* it all away, but I couldn't *keep* it away. You see, soon after I had the experience with the sky, strange things began to happen. A man hiked all the way up my mountain to give me a large sum of cash. He said that it was a dividend, or a return on a past investment, or something. He insisted that I take it." Baba chuckled to himself. "He still comes back every so often, huffing and puffing and looking rather annoyed. Then, several months later," he continued, "my old servants began trickling in here. They said that they'd rather work for me than anyone else. Before long, I was living as I had so long ago." He smiled. "Except this time I'm happy. This time, I have the proper perspective."

"But sir," the young man said, accepting the seat at the head of the table, "you're supposed to be a teacher. Do you really feel that this is the right way to live?" He looked around. "This affluently?"

Baba grinned and waved an arm at the table. "All of this helps me to appreciate the infinite. I accept it for what it is." He took a seat next to the boy. "Do you know what I learned when I saw the sky?"

Clare shook his head.

"I learned that the only things that matter are our thoughts."

"Our thoughts?"

"When I was lying up there on the roof, staring at the sky," said Baba, "I finally had a thought of

117

limitlessness. Since then, my life has been filled with limitless things. I simply accept them."

Clare looked at the table and nodded. "It *does* look pretty limitless."

"And there will be more," said Baba. "It's beautiful. Now, can we begin?"

"Well, hold on," said Clare, a little hesitantly. "First tell me what you mean about your thoughts. You didn't *think* this food into existence."

Baba laughed. "Maybe not. But then again, maybe I did."

"What do you mean?"

"Before I saw the sky, I never thought that there was enough to go around. Everything I wanted seemed out of reach."

"Out of reach? You mean, like the pastries when you were a kid?"

"Yes, like the pastries. And like everything else, really. If I had enough pastries then I didn't have enough money. If I had money, I didn't have enough friends. I always felt limited."

"Until you saw the sky," said Clare.

"Right. Until then," said Baba. "When I finally saw the sky, I let go of my belief in limits. And that's when I really began to see."

Clare nodded. "But what does that have to do with this food?"

"I never went back to thinking of limits," explained Baba. "Not after I saw the sky. And do you know what happened? My whole life began to shift. Everywhere I turned I found limitlessness—in the food, in my money, in the people around me. Even this silly old palace began to look limitlessly beautiful."

"Just because you changed your *thoughts?*"asked Clare.

Baba laughed. "I don't know how it works. But, yes—just because I changed my thoughts. When I felt limited, I never seemed to have enough. But now that I feel limitless, everything flows to me in limitless quantities. It's wonderful!" he added. Then he said, "Now—can we eat?"

Clare looked at the table. "It feels a bit too much for me," he admitted. "I mean, I've never even *seen* food like this."

"It's a gift," said Baba. "From the infinite."

"Yeah, well—still," Clare said, "I don't know if I can accept it."

Baba's shoulders sagged. He looked lovingly at the food. Then he said, "Well, OK. I think we can take a minute or two to work the limits out of you."

"Out of *me?*"protested Clare. "No—I don't think in terms of limits."

"No?" said Baba.

"No. I never looked at things like you did. I mean, I'm pretty content with everything."

"Let's see," said Baba. "I'll bet we can find some limits in you somewhere." He dashed off through a pair of doors and quickly returned with a quill pen and paper. He gave the items to Clare. "A little exercise for you. Your job is to write yourself a recommendation."

"A recommendation?" the boy asked, accepting the pen. "For what?"

"Oh," said Baba, waving his hands, "it doesn't matter. A recommendation for anything—for an award or something. But here's the catch," he said. "It has to be perfect. No limits on yourself."

Clare looked uncertainly at the man for a moment before turning to his task. He scribbled a few sentences. "How long does this have to be?" he asked.

The man laughed. "Long!" he said. "This should be the best thing anyone has ever written. Make it perfect."

Clare covered the page with lines. When he had filled the space, he asked Baba whether he should stop.

"Do you want to?" asked the man.

Clare thought for a moment. He smiled slyly. "Well . . . no," he said. "Actually, I'd rather keep going."

"Excellent!" cried Baba, and ran off to fetch another sheet of paper. When Clare was finally done with his writing, Baba picked up the pages.

"Let's see . . ." he said, reading the words, " 'I hereby recommend Clare for the Wonderful Person award—' Good," he said, "I like that. OK, let's see— 'because of the following merits: he is intelligent, and independent, and strong, and caring, and he listens well (although sometimes he argues too much).' Oh goodness," said Baba. "Already we have it."

"What?" asked Clare, shocked to hear it. "What do we have?"

"A limit. Already it has pounced. This is what I meant by the belief in limits—you slipped in a criticism. You said that you argue too much."

"But I do!" Clare protested. "And anyway, that's not necessarily a criticism," he added. "It just adds a bit of humor to the recommendation, if you read it the right way."

"Hmm . . ." said Baba. "Well, all right. Let's skim down the page." He mumbled over the words as he read them. Finally his voice climbed, articulating the words, " 'and, though he does not show brilliance in school, I do not feel that this should be held against him.' Did you need to stick that in?"

"Well, no, I suppose not. But I wanted to be honest."

Baba grinned. "All right, well, how about *this?*" he said, pointing to a spot on the page. " '. . . except for the fact that he is often impatient and tries to rush things too quickly . . .' *That* seems like a limit, pure and simple."

"Well, fine," said Clare, grabbing the paper from Baba's hands. "So maybe I can't write myself a perfect recommendation."

Baba laughed. "You know what?" he said. "Very few people can. It's part of the same game—if limits are real, then there's never enough food or money or good things to say. It's all either infinitely available, or it's not."

Clare scratched the side of his nose. He looked at the sprawling table before him. "And you think this has something to do with my attitude toward the meal," he said.

"Take a person in love with limits, set him down in a perfect world, and *he will not be able to accept it.* That's what I'm trying to show you," said Baba.

Clare looked rather uncomfortable. "It just feels like too much," he admitted.

"Ah, but *too much?*" asked the man. "What a concept!" He lovingly stroked a colorful melon. "Too much beauty?" He tore apart a loaf of bread. "Too much freshness?"

"Look," said Clare, "I guess I feel that we shouldn't use more than we need. I just don't want to waste anything."

They sat at the table for a while. Baba, looking longingly at the food, began to tap his fingers. Clare tried to figure out how to talk the man down to a more reasonable meal. "Let me tell you a little story about waste," Baba finally said. "Then—ready or not— we're going to eat.

"Once upon a time," he began, "there were two brothers. When these two brothers reached an age to go forth into the world, their father split his inheritance between them. 'Spend wisely' was all he said. Both of the brothers nodded.

"The two brothers walked together through the land until they came upon a town. At the edge of the town was a beggar. 'Can you spare anything for me?' the beggar asked them. The first brother remembered his father's words and decided that giving such gifts would be a wise way to spend the money. So he gave the beggar a generous amount. The second brother thought of his father's words and decided that giving away money was an unwise practice. He held onto his wealth.

"Before too long the brothers came upon a woman selling a mule. 'Will you buy my mule?' she asked the pair. The first brother remembered his father's guidance and decided that buying a mule was a wise way to spend his money. He bought the animal. The second brother laughed, remembering his father's words. 'My brother never was a wise one with money,' he thought to himself. 'If he keeps up like this, he'll squander his fortune within days.'

"After a while, the two brothers came upon a fruit merchant. 'Fresh apples!' the merchant cried. 'Buy my fresh apples!' The first brother led his mule up to the man and offered to buy some apples. 'How many do you want?' asked the merchant.

" 'How many would you like me to buy?' asked the first brother.

"The merchant laughed. 'Well, how about *all* of them?' he said. 'You can load them onto your mule and sell them throughout the town. That way, I can go home and rest for the afternoon.' The brother thought about this proposal and decided that it was a wise way to spend his money. So he bought all the man's apples.

" 'You fool,' said the second brother, out loud this time. 'Didn't you pay any attention to our father's guidance? He told us to *spend wisely*.'

"The first brother shrugged. 'To me, it seems like a wise enough way to spend.' He loaded the apples onto his mule. 'Would you like to come help me sell them?' he asked. The second brother only shook his head. 'I pity you, my brother,' he said. 'For you will soon be poor and hopeless. As for me, I will leave this town and not spend my money so unwisely.' And thus he left.

"As the years passed, the first brother continued to buy apples and sell them from his mule. He eventually became a much-loved distributor of fruit. He invested his profits in the businesses of his community, and together the townspeople grew prosperous. All was well in his life.

"One day, late in life, the first brother heard a knock at his door. He opened it to find a familiar beggar—a man he had not seen in many years. 'Ah,' he cried, 'it is so good to see you! But my brother,' he then said, 'where have you been these many years? And why are you so thin and pale, and why do you wear the clothes of a beggar?'

"The second brother, who now leaned in the doorway, weakly hung his head. 'I have traveled the world all these years, afraid to waste the gift of our father,' he explained. 'I misunderstood his guidance; now I am too sick and old to continue on.' He then pulled out a sack of coins. 'I haven't spent a penny of his gift. Please use it to buy me the best funeral in the world.' And with that, he died.

"Choose wisely your attitudes towards waste," concluded Baba. "Now can we eat?"

"That's an interesting story," said Clare. "But you *can't* be saying that we should spend money without regard to our supply of it."

"Oh, my dear guest!" cried Baba, apparently nearing wit's end. "Do we breathe without regard to the supply of air? Do we drink without regard to the amount of water in our glass? Of course! We neither breathe nor drink too much; we simply take what naturally comes. It's the only way to live." He picked up a small bell from the table and handed it to the boy. "Now. Shall we try?" he asked sweetly.

Clare tightened his lips in consideration and then exhaled a deep breath. Nodding, he rang the bell.

In an instant, emerging from all of the room's eight doors, men and women piled into the hall. Each took a seat at the table. All smiled and bowed their heads warmly in the direction of the two original figures.

"Clare," said Baba by way of introduction, "my fellow servants. They have created this for you."

Quickly, a man sprang from his seat and presented the guest with a bottle of wine. "Your approval?" he asked. Clare nodded self-consciously. The steward then opened the bottle and poured a scant amount into the young man's glass. "Please taste it," he requested. Clare obeyed and gave another slight nod. The man smiled. Rushing around the room, opening six bottles in total, he filled each person's glass.

When the man was done, a woman sprang up energetically and served each person two slices of bread. The dance went on; each of the servants performed part of the ritual. After a few bites of the dinner, Clare was forced to admit that the offering was glorious.

During the course of the meal, the steward taught him the proper method of drinking wine. ("You must tickle it with the tip of your tongue," he instructed, eyes ablaze with satisfaction.) At the end, the dessert chef insisted that he try each of the featured pastries. ("It's a tradition here," she explained with a wink toward Baba.) By the end of the dinner, Clare felt quite warm and comforted. Somewhat chagrined, he realized that the elaborate meal was simply a way for the servants to offer their generous goodwill.

"You were right, I was wrong," he admitted to his grinning host after the dinner had been cleared away and the company had departed. "The meal was perfect."

"As is *every* meal," said Baba with a satisfied sigh.

ॐ

"I suppose that the real issue is this," said Baba later that evening. "The belief in limits leads right to judgment. And judgment makes such a mess of the world." Baba and Clare were now seated on couches in a comfortable sitting room. The ceilings weren't as high here, and Clare was beginning to feel a little more relaxed. "It's really so unnecessary," the man added.

"Judging people, you mean?"

"Yes, people. And everything else." Baba leaned back on his couch. "You know, at the moment I saw the sky, a great idea hit me: I saw that I never again had to set things right."

Clare looked puzzled.

"I saw that everything is OK, that the whole universe is just fine," continued the man. "I saw that I didn't need to fix anything. It was quite a relief."

"What were you trying to fix in the first place?"

"Just about everything," said Baba. "When I was an orphan, the food needed to be fixed. When I was working in the bakery, the desserts needed to be fixed. After that, I needed to fix the world with my money." Baba sat up again. "But when I saw the sky, I realized that I could let all of my judgments go."

"You know," said Clare, "I sort of follow you. But what do judgments have to do with fixing things?"

"It's judgments that keep us in a world of problems," said Baba.

"But what kind of judgments? You don't mean personal judgments—like where we should go, or how we should act . . . "

"Or what we should eat," added Baba.

"Yeah. Things like that. I mean, you can't live without making them."

"No?"

"Of course not. If we didn't make judgments, we'd just sit around. There'd be nothing to do."

"Nothing to do except *appreciate*," smiled Baba.

"Well, that sounds pretty boring to me," said Clare.

Baba laughed. "I suppose it does. But let me ask you this: Haven't you ever lived in a perfect world? One which seemed magical at times?"

"Yeah, maybe I did once," said the boy with a smile, recalling some happy memories, "but I outgrew it."

"No," said Baba. "You did as we all do. You began to judge it."

"Judge it?"

Baba nodded. "But the secret is that it's still right in front of you. And it's easy to get back to," he added. "All you need to do is release your judgments. You just have to accept the possibility that everything in your life is perfectly fine."

"Wait a minute," said Clare, shaking his head. "You're telling me I should just sit around all day? Without making any decisions about anything?"

"No, no," Baba said, chuckling. "I suppose we all need to make *decisions*. But you can make decisions without judging the world. You can do what you want to do without saying, 'This is good and that is bad.'"

Clare frowned. "I really don't see how."

"It's easy," said Baba. "All you need to do is listen to the master."

"The master?" said Clare. "Where does *he* fit in?"

"He fits in everywhere. For he is you."

Clare blinked his eyes in surprise. "*I'm* the master?"

"Indeed."

"Well, that doesn't make much sense," sputtered Clare. "I mean, I came here because I thought *you* were the master. But then you told me there's only one master. And now you're telling me that *I'm* the master?"

"You are," nodded Baba, "I am. Everyone is."

"We're all masters?"

"Yes."

Clare was confused. "Well, then why don't we go around knowing everything? And being perfectly happy and all?"

"We will," said Baba. "As soon as we see the sky."

Clare shook his head. "I don't get it."

"We're all masters," said the man. "Perhaps we don't see it yet. But the more we act like masters, the more we realize who we are."

Clare scratched his head. "So we can *practice* it? Is that what you're saying?"

"Exactly. The key is this: when you're making a decision—any kind of decision—just believe that you're infinitely powerful. Believe it for an instant, and—whoosh! Your answer comes."

Clare looked at the man. "Infinitely powerful?"

"Infinitely. Just like a master. Infinitely knowledgeable. Infinitely creative. Infinitely at peace."

"Well, I don't see how believing something like that will help me to make decisions . . . "

"But it will!" insisted Baba. "Try it. It gives you the proper perspective on the world. Look at the decisions you've made so far in your life—I bet a lot of them weren't decisions that a master would make."

"Maybe," said Clare. "But so what?"

"So that's what's kept you from realizing the truth: you *are* the master." Baba thought to himself for a moment. "Shall we try an experiment?"

Clare rubbed his eyebrows. "Not another recommendation," he said.

"No," laughed Baba. "This time your task is to choose a profession. Let's say you're about to go forth in the world, and you have a thousand possibilities. You can become a pastry chef or a fisherman or an innkeeper or anything else you can dream up. What will you choose?"

Clare waited for a few seconds. "You want me to choose *now?*"

"Yes," said the man, "like a master."

"Well," decided Clare after a moment, "I always thought that owning a store would be a pretty smart thing to do. I mean, everyone needs to buy things. Right?"

"And is that what you'd do if you woke up one day and realized that you were the master?" asked Baba. "Would you own a store if you found that you were infinitely wise, infinitely strong, and infinitely wealthy?"

Clare reflected. "No, I suppose not. I might do something else then."

"Like what?"

The young man thought and thought. Finally he said, "Well, I might be a gardener or something. That is, if I didn't need to worry about anything else. I might grow a garden—like I used to at home."

Baba smiled and opened his arms. "The master has spoken."

"But I'm not a master!" Clare said emphatically. "And I *do* need to worry about other things."

Baba threw his head back and laughed. "My dear guest—you know a master's thoughts. Who else could you be?"

Clare and his host sat in silence on the couches for a while. Finally, with a smile, Baba took Clare's hand and led him to a comfortable bedroom. "Sleep well," he requested.

∾

"I'm so glad to have a guest," admitted Baba the next morning. "It's been a while since anyone's hiked up here."

"Yeah. I'm glad I came," said Clare. The two were back in the high-ceilinged atrium, sitting on pillows. Baba had fetched another pot of tea from behind his chair; now he was pouring. "But you know," added Clare with a rather dejected look, "I have no idea what I should do now."

"Drink your tea," said Baba, offering him a cup.

"Thanks," said Clare. "But I mean about my journey. I've been traveling for so long, and I'm not any closer to finding my father than when I began." He shook his head. "Maybe I should have stayed home."

Baba laughed. "Yes, maybe," he said. "But maybe not. You know, a journey is a funny thing."

Clare looked up. "How's that?"

"Journeys sometimes end as soon as we're ready for them to end. At least, that's what happened for me—when I was ready to find the sky, I did. And when I was ready to have a father, that came too."

"But I don't know where he is. He could be *any-where*."

"Does the master want to find him?"

"You mean, if I were infinitely powerful and all that, would I still want to find him?" Clare didn't need to think about it. "Yeah. I would. I'd do whatever it takes. I still need to ask him some questions."

Baba nodded. "Well, I've been waiting to do this," he said. Then he added, "He came yesterday—he said he had a message—but I wanted to spend a little time with you first." Baba then took a bell from the tea tray and rang it.

"Who came?" asked Clare. In response to his question, a single man entered from the great double doors. Clare looked at the man closely, watching him approach. Then he jumped to his feet in horror. Before him stood the red-mustached man he had met on the road.

The boy's eyes darted to Baba. Was this a trick? He couldn't believe what he was seeing. "This man tried to rob me!" the boy announced angrily, pointing a finger. "Just when I was beginning my journey. He tried to take everything I owned."

Baba nodded at the outburst, but nevertheless invited the visitor to join them. The man looked different from when Clare had first met him; now his face seemed gentler, more open. "This man can help you find your father," explained Baba.

Clare, still breathing heavily, opened his eyes in surprise. "What?" he cried. "No way."

"Infinitely trusting," reminded Baba with a wink. "Remember, you're the master."

"Well, fine," said Clare after a moment of struggle. Then, scowling, he asked the man, "How can you help me?"

"I sit at the crossroads and listen," the red-mustached man told him. "I hear a lot of stories."

"What kinds of stories?"

"Stories of journeys. Stories of searches. Some people sit with me for a while and tell me about themselves; others just hurry on down the road."

"Look," said Clare, feeling a bit needled, "you were going to *rob* me."

The man laughed. "Who knows? Maybe I was. Then again, maybe I could have been your greatest guide."

Clare shielded his mouth with the back of his hand. "Do you *know* this guy?" he whispered to Baba.

Baba laughed. "He shows up here from time to time."

"Well, what do you know about my father?" Clare asked, turning back to the red-mustached man. "Have you spoken to him?"

"No," said the man. "But I've heard many stories lately—stories of a great teacher. People are walking the roads, seeking this person for guidance. They say he has awakened, as if from a dream. I think he may be your father."

Clare's head snapped back in surprise. "Why do you say that?"

"The legends have already taken shape. They say he was once a great leader—he had wealth, and a wife and son. But for the sake of the world, he left his home to seek the truth. Now he has found it."

Clare paused. "And so where is he, this teacher?"

"People are traveling toward him on the old western road. They say he has a camp by the sea. That's all I know."

The boy sat for a moment, absorbing the information. "And you came here to tell me this?" he asked.

"I have heard of you, too," the man explained. "I've heard about your journey—I knew where to find you."

Clare raised his eyebrows. "Well, thank you, I guess," he said. "I'll think about what you said."

The man smiled—almost warmly now, it seemed. He rose, bowed to Baba, and quickly left through the doors from which he had entered.

"I think you know that guy better than you were letting on," Clare said after a minute.

Baba laughed. "You're right. He's a master."

Clare threw his hands in the air. "Of course—I should have known."

"You'll find masters everywhere, if you just keep your eyes open."

"Well, anyway," said Clare, "something tells me to trust what that guy told me. I'm telling you, he *did* try to rob me. At least, I think. But he seems more honest now. Besides—I don't have anything else to go on."

"Then go on a master's faith," said Baba. "Right to your father."

FIVE

The sea. It surpassed every one of his dreams.

Back home, Clare had wondered what the sea would look like. He had pieced together an idea from pictures in his schoolbooks and reports from the marketplace. He had settled on an image. But it turned out to be nothing like the sea.

The sea was huge. It was alive. It was wider than anything the boy had seen, and it never stopped moving. It rose and fell back upon itself. It hit the rocky shores with a crash. It blew forth clouds of misty fog which danced in the air above it. The sea stretched for miles, until it met the sky, and even then it didn't stop.

As a child, Clare had once heard a fable of a proud river. This river ran its way across the land, giving its valuable water to some while denying it to others. The river imagined itself supreme king of the land—until the day it found the sea. On that day, the river saw both its master and its destination.

Now, as Clare stood and marveled at the sea, he knew what the river had seen.

∾

A few weeks earlier, having heard about the teacher by the sea, the boy had packed his things and waved farewell to Baba. Somehow he knew that this teacher was the person he sought.

For weeks Clare walked west with the sun, finding his shadow laid out before him, then below him, then stretching behind. At one point he picked up a ragged straw hat from the road and stuck it onto his head. He wondered if it might have belonged to someone else who also sought this great teacher by the sea.

As he walked, Clare tried to imagine what the meeting with his father would be like. He rehearsed all the things he wanted to tell him. He made a list of the questions to ask. He drew a mental picture of the water, the seagulls, and the camp full of people.

In his mind's eye he saw his father standing before a group, the setting sun at his back. The man was nothing but a silhouette, a vague shape that floated among the crowd. He was sharing the wisdom his search had unearthed. He was giving the people his gift. And he seemed truly happy.

Clare frowned. The dream made him feel rather unimportant. He kicked a stone with the toe of his boot and thought about his journey. Why do I care so much about finding him? he wondered. And what could he possibly say to me? Clare tried to envision a man with a face and a heart, but every time the shadow figure returned.

Eventually he gave up trying to imagine the meeting. He was going to the sea, to find his father—whatever the outcome. Clare walked resolutely for many miles, through many days on the open road, and finally he felt the cool shore mist. Minutes later, he found the sea.

The sea—what power it had. What grace, too; and what a glorious crash it made against the rocks. Clare slowly shook his head, clearing away the old images forever. This was it, the huge and wonderful sea. *This* was a place to end one's journey. He smiled and was glad.

The road twisted course here and unrolled along the top of a cliff. Below it crashed the waves. Clare strolled along the edge, watching lizards and chattering birds run before his footsteps. He shook his head again. For here was the sea he'd dreamed of, and here *must* be his father, and here he felt ready for anything.

Clare walked for hours, taking in the sights. A pair of hawks teetered in the air currents. A line of pine trees skirted the path. Grassy meadows appeared from time to time, and once he saw a deer. He stepped lightly between the prickly ground plants; he listened for the wind. But not once did he see another soul.

He walked in silence. And as he walked, his thoughts turned back over the whole of his journey. Clare recalled his first step on the road. He remembered being thrown in a ditch and waking up to meet Samara. He remembered Jing and the river, and Baba in the mountains. He thought of his mother back home in her garden. He smiled at the whole thing, for it seemed suddenly perfect.

And then a great light dawned.

In an instant it came and went, but for that instant it was there: the vision for which Clare had been born. He finally, thoroughly saw. He saw the waves and the afternoon sky. He saw the rocky cliffs. He saw himself, and every one of his steps, and suddenly he saw: *my answer is here.* Suddenly he knew it: *right here is my answer—at my fingertips, in the air. It always was and it always will be.* He paused, looked out across the sea, and was filled with a deep sense of peace.

"Beautiful sight, isn't it?" said a woman's voice unexpectedly. Clare turned rather slowly to meet it.

"Yes," he agreed, nodding his head to a gypsylike figure. Her clothes were covered in patches. Her arms were wrapped in bangles.

"Have you come to see the Awakened One?" She asked it like that—capital letters and all.

Clare smiled. He decided that he was in the right place. "I've heard that a great teacher is here. I came to speak to him. Do you know anything about this?"

She laughed spiritedly. "Of course! He's the reason we've all come."

"All?" Clare asked. "How many of you are there?"

She counted in her head. "Perhaps twenty. Soon there will be more—his story is spreading fast."

"So you've met him?"

"Yes," she beamed, recalling something sweet. "He came through my village one day. He walked into town with a beggar's bowl and sat with the poor people. He began to talk to them—about things like truth and vision, and the true meaning of life. Before long, the whole town was out there—beggars and rich folk and all—listening to him speak. I knew he was telling us the truth. I just knew it."

"So you followed him?"

"Yes. He said he was traveling to the sea, to wait for something. He told us that we could come with him."

Clare asked, "So does he speak to you? I mean, does he sit and teach you things?"

"No," she replied. "Not really. He's pretty quiet most of the time. I guess that he's more of a guide than anything else."

"But you said he's awake," said Clare. "What does that mean? Does he have some kind of special power?"

She shrugged. "I don't know. It really doesn't matter, though—you'll know what I mean when you meet him. It's just something in his eyes."

The young man hitched his pack on to his shoulders. "Will you show me where he is?"

"Sure," she said. "Follow me."

She led him down a path that sloped on to an outcrop of rock. As they approached the site, Clare began to make out a collection of simple shelters. She pointed. "We're building these—just a temporary thing, really. You can help if you want." She smiled and left to attend to another project.

There were many people milling around here; they seemed to come from all walks of life. Young and old, rich and poor—all were working to build the little wooden structures. "A new one, hey?" said a gruff-looking man who was digging a hole. A smile then cracked his face. "Welcome, youngster," he followed with a handshake.

"Hi," said Clare, walking over to him. "I'm looking for this person they call the Awakened One."

"Well," laughed the man. "That's a pretty impressive title for such a humble fellow."

"But you know who I'm talking about . . . "

"Of course! He's the reason we're here."

"So what do *you* call him?"

The man leaned on his shovel. "Well, everyone seems to call him something different. To me, he's just 'friend.' That's all. Quite a friend, though, I must say."

Clare nodded. "Did you hear him speak one day? Is that how you met him?"

The man laughed. "It's more like I *felt* him speak. You see, I had heard people talk about a man who was stronger than a hundred other men. I decided to check it out. I followed the stories until I caught up with him in a little clearing in the forest. He only had five or six people with him back then.

"Anyway," the man continued, "he was pretty small in person—I laughed at first. I went up to him and said, 'I hear you're pretty powerful.' He didn't say anything for a while; he just looked me in the eye. Then he said, 'Someday you'll learn about real power.' And then do you know what happened?"

Clare shook his head.

"Right then a gust of wind blew by, and it snapped off a tree branch, and the thing fell *right at my feet*. I mean, it *was* windy that day, but it happened just when he said that. 'Someday you'll learn about real power.' When that happened, nothing could stop me from joining him."

The boy frowned. "That really happened?"

"I've never seen anything else like it. Stuff happens when you're around him—other people have seen it, too. He's a pretty powerful fellow."

"But you said humble, too."

"That's exactly it. You've never seen a more gentle man." He waved his hands. "Look, I can't describe it. You just need to see it for yourself."

"Well, where is he?" asked Clare. "Does he have a cabin or something?"

The man thought for a minute. "I don't know. He just wanders around. He's waiting for something— then we're all going to a really great place. You might try looking for him down by the water."

"Thanks," said Clare.

"Good luck," said the man, and he returned to his work.

Clare worked his way across the rocks, climbing out toward the water's edge. The spray from the crashing waves fanned through the air here; it clung against his skin, cool and alive.

He wondered a bit at this cliff-side collection of people. Why would they all leave their homes to follow a man with a beggar's bowl? Was he really all that great? Clare began to feel a bit nervous about his meeting with the man. Would the great teacher mean anything to him?

He scrambled over the seaside boulders, searching for movement, but he found nothing. Finally he climbed out onto a rock that anchored an old and twisted tree.

He sat in its shade, overlooking the curling waves. The water rose upon a half-submerged boulder here, hanging steady for a moment; then it drained down the side in a thousand little waterfalls. Clare watched the show, his eyes growing heavy. Soon he dropped off to sleep.

After a while, he heard voices—or a voice—in a dream, and realized that he was half-awake. He opened his eyes to find a weather-beaten face before him. "I hear that you're looking for the ol' man," said the person.

Clare pushed himself into a sitting position. "Yeah," he said sleepily, blinking his eyes awake. "Do you know where he is?"

"Sure," said the other. "But why do you want to find him? I don't think he's such a big deal."

Clare raised his eyebrows. He examined the matted locks of hair, the aged skin and tattered clothes of this fellow before him. "You're the first one I've met who's said that. Everyone else is quite taken with him."

"Well," said the man, plopping down in the shade next to Clare, "I've seen a lot of people and a lot of things. It's all about the same to me."

"Really."

"Oh, sure," he said casually. "Hey, look out there," he added, pointing a finger. "Pelicans."

Clare turned and saw a group of strange-looking birds fly by. "So what's your story, then?" he asked. "Why are you here, if not to see the great teacher?"

"My story *is* my story," explained the man with a laugh. "You see, I'm a storyteller. That's what I do. I came here for the stories."

"The stories?"

"Sure! Everyone has a tale or two to tell. Probably more than that, in fact. I listen, and I tell them." He pointed a thumb back toward the camp. "There's a lot of interesting stories back there."

Clare nodded. "I believe it. I've heard quite a few on my trip." He decided that he liked this ragged fellow—the man seemed so human.

"Oh," he said, interested. "You're on a trip? To where?"

"Well," began Clare, "I once knew this great man who everyone is talking about. When I was really young, that is. I haven't seen him for a long time."

"Sounds like there could be a good story there," remarked the man.

Clare smiled a little. "Yeah. Anyway, I'm here to see him. But I guess there's no rush—I mean, I've been traveling for a long time."

"Traveling from far away?"

"Yes. Really far. You know what, though?" he said. "When I finally got to the sea, I almost felt as if I had never left. I sort of knew that my answer was *everywhere.* And that I had just been wandering around for fun."

The man nodded slowly, considering this. "*Was* it fun?" he asked.

"Well, not all the time. But in the end, I think I'll look at it that way. For now I'm done."

The man shifted his position so that his face caught the warmth of the sun. "And then you're going to go back home? After you find what you came here for?"

"Maybe. Though I might just find a new home of my own. I'm learning to trust what turns up."

"Sounds good," said the man.

"Yeah. Now, how about these stories of yours? Do you want to tell me one?"

The man looked both pleased and surprised. "Now?" he asked. "Right here?"

"Sure," agreed Clare. "It's a good day for a story."

The man laughed. "It is indeed." He straightened himself. "OK, here's a little one for you. If you don't like it, you won't be put off for too long."

Clare nodded and settled against his tree. Then his companion began.

∾

"Once there was a warrior, arrogant and strong," said the man. His voice was serious now; his words almost hung in the air. Clare decided that he took his storytelling very seriously. The man continued: "This

143

warrior's legs were like columns of stone. His chest was hard as a boulder. He was tougher than anyone around, and he never missed an opportunity to prove it.

"People hurried out of his way as he walked through the streets. They sighed with relief when he left to do battle. The warrior issued a single challenge to everyone he met: 'Bow before me, you worm, or face your death!' For years, everyone bowed.

"Then, one hot summer day, his challenge was answered. While sauntering through the middle of town, the warrior was struck in the chest by an arrow. A terrible cry tore from his throat. All but one of the village crowd scattered.

"The single person who remained was a white-bearded gentleman. He crept up to the warrior and explained, 'I'm a surgeon. Please let me remove that arrow for you.'

"The warrior spat on the man. 'No one will touch this until I have my revenge,' he swore. The warrior then ripped the arrow from his chest and held it in the air. He cried to the hidden townsfolk, 'I will carry this arrow until I know the name of the man who shot it at me, the names of his brothers, and the place where he lives.' He turned to face the other side of the town. 'I will carry this puny thing until I know the blacksmith who forged its tip and the craftsman who carved its shaft.' His face tightened in rage. 'I will know this all!' he bellowed, *and I will have my revenge!*'

"Now by this time even the meek old doctor had scuttled out of sight, and the wounded man found himself alone in the marketplace. The echoes of his promise scattered into the neighboring hills. Gritting his teeth with resolution, the warrior began his journey.

"Needless to say, his chosen quest was not an easy one. From the wound came a steady trickle of blood which stained the ground below him. The warrior's strength gradually ebbed; only the will of a battle-worn fighter kept his limbs locked to their march. He had visited only a pair of blacksmiths when his legs buckled and he dropped to his knees. But the warrior crushed all thoughts of defeat and continued his search in a crawl.

"Days passed as the warrior crawled along the road. Suns and moons rose and fell, but the man saw only his goal. He knew that his thirst for vengeance would eventually be quenched.

"However, there came a time when the ground swirled and the sky threw down its weight. With a choke and a gasp, the warrior finally fell.

"Birds of prey soon gathered around his motionless body, testing for life with their cries. The warrior didn't move. Just as the boldest of the scavengers was about to claim a piece of flesh, an old man came scurrying up the road.

"He scattered the birds with several yells and a few choice pebbles; then he turned to attend to the body. He gingerly opened the warrior's shirt, cleaned his wound, and bandaged his chest with some cloth. He then covered the warrior with his own coat and seated himself upon the ground in a protective vigil. After a day the warrior awoke. 'You saved me,' he said, recognizing the old village doctor.

" 'Yes,' smiled the doctor. 'I've been following you.' He patted a large shoulder. 'Just rest now.'

" 'Where's the arrow?' asked the warrior.

" 'It's next to you,' the doctor said.

" 'I will have you know,' said the warrior coldly as he reached for the arrow, 'that when I'm able, I will tear open this wound and continue my search.'

" 'And I,' said the old man, his voice soft with years, 'will continue to follow you.' "

"That's a strange story," said Clare when the man's voice had trailed off into the distance.

"It was good for me to hear that one," said the storyteller. "I used to be just like that warrior."

"Mean like him?"

"No. Not mean. But I was just as determined to find what I wanted. Blindly determined at times." Then he said, "You know, I think there's only two ways to walk through life—like the warrior or like the old doctor."

"You mean, we can hurt people or we can help them."

The man nodded his head. "Yeah. I think that most of us start out like the warrior. We're not out to *kill* anyone, maybe, but we're certainly not there to help anyone, either. We're on a personal mission."

"And you think that type of life falls apart after a while?" asked Clare. "Like the warrior fell?"

"Exactly—that's a good way to put it. It just falls apart. *We* fall apart. Then a doctor comes along, and we have a choice: we can accept his help or we can keep fighting our fight. If we accept the healing, we become healers ourselves."

Clare thought about it for a while. "And is that what happened to you, too? Did you make that change?"

"I did," nodded the man. "I began my journey all alone, with the wound of a fighter, and I fell many times along my way. It's only recently that I've begun to see the obvious: *every* warrior is wounded. And the only other way to live is as a healer."

"So it's either one or the other. Nothing in between."

"I don't know. I guess there *was* a transition period of sorts. But for me, it was pretty dramatic. Here I was—a warrior, a hero on a quest—collapsing over and over until I couldn't go on. The only way I could get up that last time was to change my focus. So I started helping people."

"Helping through storytelling?"

The man laughed. "I guess it does sound strange, but somehow that was the way it worked out."

Clare nodded his head in thought. "That's a bit like my story, too. I began my journey alone and I pretty quickly ended up in a ditch. Ever since then, I've been learning things. Maybe I'll find a way to help out someday."

"I'm sure you will," said the man.

The boy thought about the story. "But there seems to be another meaning there, too. The warrior wanted to know all those things—like who shot him and who made the arrow. Do you think that's part of the warrior's way? Looking for answers?"

"Good question. I don't know. It didn't seem like the old doctor needed any answers, though. He knew what to do with his life."

"He just wanted to help out."

The man nodded. "Help and heal. That was it."

Clare propped himself up on the rock a bit. "Well, that story was interesting enough," he said. "Do you have any others?"

"Enough to keep you up all night, I bet." The man looked at him suspiciously. "But are you sure you want to hear another one? You're not just being polite?"

Clare laughed. "No, really; let's have another one." He was having fun with this fellow by the edge of the sea.

"Short or long this time?"

"How about a long one."

The man thought; then he nodded and began.

∾

"Once there was a monk who wandered from town to town seeking alms. Although he usually slept on a stable floor and his clothes were nothing more than a tatter of patches, he lived a happy life. His days were peaceful. The gifts from the townspeople kept him well fed. The trees shielded him from the rain and the streams spoke to him as he bathed in their waters. All in all, the monk was content.

"Now," said the storyteller, "this monk was also a very educated man. He loved to help people in need. Shopkeepers borrowed his arithmetic skills. Students struggling with their lessons sought his assistance. Every so often he'd be asked to write down a letter from one young lover to another. The monk never accepted payment for his help; he always gently refused, saying, 'Please keep your money. The life I lead is one of service.' Wherever he passed, people smiled and shook their heads, for they loved the wandering servant.

"Now, one evening the monk walked to the edge of an unfamiliar town. It was an early summer evening, dry and warm, and the monk decided to camp in a meadow at the town's border. He settled down to sleep and wished himself some pleasant dreams.

"As he slept, the moon traveled over the meadow. The monk slept soundly. Then, just before the break of dawn, he began to dream. In his dream there appeared before him a room built of marble, with crystal-blue fountains and banners waving in the breeze. Each of the banners sported a royal-looking crest. In his dream, the monk walked toward the largest fountain and washed his face in its water.

"As the ripples faded from the pool's surface, an image came into focus. There, reflected in the water of the fountain, was the face of a beautiful prince.

"The monk felt a flash of surprise. Then came a flood of memories. In his dream, the monk recalled castle-side picnics, fox-hunting expeditions, and long hours of royal tutoring. There were battles and ceremonies and magnificent tournaments. Each memory built upon the next until a whole history was in place.

"In his dream the monk then removed his silk robes and put on a set of traveling clothes. Finally he walked out of the room into the world outside.

"And at that point, our monk awoke to the light of day.

"Life in the land was just beginning to stir, but the monk sat bolt upright in the meadow. Images of his dream still lingered before his eyes, melting into the landscape before him. He slowly cast his glance over his clothes. Then he asked, 'Where am I?' Memories of fox hunts and picnics danced alongside scenes from the life of a holy man. Rubbing his temples, he finally laughed to himself.

" 'What a dream!' he said. As he collected his possessions from the dew-speckled meadow, he chuckled once again. 'Imagine!' he mumbled. 'Me as a monk!'"

"Wait," interrupted Clare, tearing his eyes from the sea. "You're saying that he had forgotten who he was?"

"We shall see," said the man mysteriously, and continued. "As our wanderer walked into the town, he was overcome by confusion. Why was he here? And where was home? He remembered leaving to go on a journey, but he couldn't remember the destination. Or the way back, come to think of it. He searched the pockets of his cloak and found nothing—no money, papers, or possessions of any sort. A moment of fear came over him, but he quickly shook it off. 'Ah well,' he said resolutely. 'Even in a traveler's cloak, a prince is still a prince.'

"He marched straight into the heart of the town, determined to reveal his identity with care. He noticed a bank near the town's center, and quickly decided upon a plan.

"Mustering his fullest stature, he strode into the bank and requested a conference with the chief banker himself. 'Why should I speak with you?' barked a gruff man from behind a desk.

" 'It will be worth your while,' replied the wanderer. His voice left little room for doubt.

"The banker frowned and impatiently ushered his visitor into a back chamber. 'So what do you want?' he said.

" 'I have an important secret to share with you,' said our former monk, taking a seat. 'Although my appearance may be deceiving, I am actually a prince in need of assistance. I assure you that your cooperation will be richly rewarded.'

"The banker scoffed at the man's words. 'Any fool can see that you wear the clothes of a beggar,' he said.

'I didn't earn my fortune lending money to beggars, and I don't intend to do so now.'

" 'Sir,' the newcomer said, 'I respect your caution. However, I will prove my identity to you. Please ask one of your clerks to join us.' The banker looked at him suspiciously, but he consented to the request. 'Now please give us an arithmetic problem or two,' said the wanderer. 'I promise to beat your clerk every time.' The banker invented a few difficult challenges, which the man solved with lightning speed. After that, he read and interpreted legal codes, balanced a ledger, and wrote out a letter of credit. Before long, the man in beggar's clothes had convinced the entire bookkeeping staff of his princely status. Only the banker remained doubtful.

" 'You're certainly not as you seem,' he admitted. 'But how am I to know that you are really a wealthy prince?'

" 'I think you will have no more doubts,' said the man, 'when you hear of my home.' At this, he leaned forward in his chair and described to his audience the details of his castle—the white marble halls, the fountains, and all the other vivid and colorful sights he remembered. The man spoke for almost an hour, describing a vision which was as clear as day. Finally the banker raised his hand.

" 'You have certainly demonstrated your worth, my lord,' he said. 'No sane man would doubt the truth of your words. You may borrow however much you wish from me, and I will have the town prepare a suitable reception.'

"Our newfound prince accepted a hefty sum of gold from the banker. The town buzzed with the news of their visitor. A tailor gave him a new suit of clothes, and a great celebratory feast was prepared.

"When finally he had been washed and fitted in his new clothes, the prince's true identity was clear. 'How could I have doubted him?' the banker asked himself as he watched the guest distribute money to the poor. 'He is as noble as he is handsome. A true prince!'

"The visitor stayed in the town for many months, accepting gifts from the people and showering them with his presence. At the end of a year's time, he decided to settle on the outskirts of town.

"He fell in love with a grocer's daughter during the following spring, and together they announced their engagement to be married. The community could barely contain its joy. By the end of the second year, he with his wife and newborn son were living happily in the midst of a devoted citizenry.

"The years passed, the prince aged, and as time went on a curious thing took place: the prince began to develop a deep appreciation for nature. He took more walks. He listened to the birds. One day he even decided to spend a night under the stars.

"The prince spoke to no one of his plan. Quietly he stole from his sleeping wife's side and crept into a moonlit pasture. The prince smiled at the tiny stars as he laid his head upon the grass.

"While he slept, the man dreamed a wondrous dream. In the depths of his sleep, he became a prince with a wife and a son and a charming little palace. His treasury was filled with riches; his subjects adored him. It was a beautiful dream, and when the man awoke, his face was lit with a wistful smile. 'Ah,' he chuckled to himself, feeling the warmth of the morning sun. 'What a funny little dream! Imagine that—me as a prince!'"

Clare sat, saying nothing for a while. "And so what happened to him, this monk-prince?" he finally asked.

The storyteller thought about it. "I think they say he made a pretty wise decision in the end."

Clare frowned; then he scratched his chin. "But I don't understand the whole sleeping and dreaming thing. How can you believe you're someone else?"

"Well, that's just it," said the man, leaning forward. "This story's about *identities*. We forget who we really are sometimes."

"Like the monk did."

"And like the prince did, too."

"So who was he really?"

"I guess that's the real question to ask. You know, I call myself a storyteller and you call yourself a young man on a journey. But who are we really?"

"Not those?"

"I don't think so," said the man, shaking his head. "Not really. I think that we're something greater. Something much greater than those."

Clare looked puzzled. "Maybe you're right. But I sure *feel* like a young man on a journey."

"I like to tell that story because it shows that our identities are like dreams," the man said. "In fact, they *are* dreams of a sort. They shift and change with time. They feel real while we're in them, but eventually we wake up."

"To what?"

"To who we really are."

"And that's something greater than monks or princes," guessed Clare. "Or storytellers or people on journeys."

"I think so," said the man. "And our job is to figure out who it is that we really are."

Clare nodded. "OK," he said. "Any more stories?"

The storyteller smiled. "One more. Then you better attend to your business here."

"Agreed."

And the man began.

∾

"Long ago, on a cold winter's night, a child was born by the light of a fire. His skin shone with a halo of warmth. The evening air about him seemed to glow. 'Our son is not ordinary,' whispered his father, edging through the shadows toward his wife. A promise then tore from his throat. 'He will be a leader among men. You will see.' The mother nodded in simple agreement. She knew her husband was right.

"Now, in time this child *did* prove to have a rather unique gift: he loved to dance. Every minute of the day he danced. Inside, outside—wherever he was, he danced. He spent most of his time in the meadows by his house, for there he could sway with the tall, sweeping grasses, twirl with the floating milkweed puffs, bounce free through the air like the hopping insects. His life was a dance, and he lived it to the fullest.

" 'Now, Bodie,' said his father rather sternly one day (for that was the child's name), 'you must not spend so much of your time alone in the fields. We have the highest hopes for you, and there's much work to be done.'

"So with an obedient sigh, the boy turned to all the strange tasks his father set before him. There were

154

leg-strengthening exercises, agility drills, and weird postures to encourage flexibility. He practiced gymnastics of the mind as well, and received lengthy instruction in methods of reasoning. The young Bodie performed his chores dutifully. Then, with a nod from his proud parent, he rushed back to the dance.

"The little one's first competition came when he was six. A footrace was being held in a neighboring town, and the father gave his son the instructions. 'All you have to do is run to that line,' said the man, pointing toward the distance. 'Show them who you really are!' The boy nodded happily, sharing in the man's excitement. When a loud voice cried 'Go!' and all the other children dashed away, little Bodie paused for a moment. Then, eyes closed, he began to slide, twirl, and spin toward the destination.

"When his dance was over, the child found a strangely disappointed look in his father's eyes. 'It's all right,' said the man, patting the boy's shoulder. 'Next time we'll do better.'

"Over the next few weeks, Bodie learned about first and last places. He learned their order and their importance. And he resolved to strive for the appointed goal, however strange it seemed to be.

"When the next race came, he tucked his head down and carried his little legs as quickly as they would go. 'See!' shouted his overjoyed father. 'I knew you could do it!' The child still didn't fully understand, but he was happy to see the smiles.

"As the young Bodie matured, he grew in stature. His limbs became strong under the regimen his father prescribed. His desire to win turned strong as well. In time, under his discipline of practice, he became a champion runner. Only on a rare Sunday afternoon would the young man retreat to a field and spin himself to rest.

"The years passed, and Bodie found that he could apply his intensity to activities beyond running. Whether riding horses, hammering nails, or solving equations, he used every ounce of his energy. He always strove for first place—and he became a champion at everything he did. 'You are a leader among men,' said his father one day. 'Just like I knew you would be.'

"In time Bodie became a quite powerful man. His influence spread over the land. People held his opinion in high esteem, and many approached him for advice. Bodie worked diligently to serve the people who sought his help. Not once did he fail to find a solution to their problems.

"Now," said the storyteller, "one day when Bodie was walking through the countryside, he came across a man by the side of the road. The man was very old, and he was sitting all by himself. 'Sir,' said Bodie, 'Why are you sitting here? Can I help you with anything?'

"The man shook his head. 'No,' he said. 'No one can help me now. I'm just waiting to die.'

" 'To *die?*' said Bodie. 'But why?'

" 'I am so old,' said the man, 'that I have nothing left in the world. My family is gone. My body is weak. Even my home has fallen apart.'

"Bodie was shocked. 'But sir!' he said, 'you have to keep going! You can't give up on your life like this.'

"The old man smiled and shook his head again. He said, 'There comes a time when we all must go. My time is now.'

"Bodie couldn't persuade the man to come with him; at long last, he simply had to leave. But day after day Bodie came back to the man's spot and tried to convince him to return to the town. Every day the man refused. Bodie watched the old man's health gradually deteriorate, until one morning he arrived to find a lifeless body. He stared at it for a while. Then he made a declaration. 'I will find an answer to this,' he said. 'Life cannot possibly be so meaningless.'

"Bodie searched for an answer in every place he knew. And as he searched he began to notice how people around him struggled. He began to understand their feelings of loss. And he redoubled his commitment to help.

"Then, one day, he could no longer wait. He knew his answer was somewhere out there; and he knew he needed to find it. So he left his home.

"He wandered over the lands for many years, questioning every wise man and woman who crossed his path. 'Do you have the answer?' he wanted to know. 'What is the meaning of this life?' Many people tried to help, but none provided him with a satisfactory answer.

"The years passed, and Bodie began to doubt that he'd ever find his answer. He grew lonely, discouraged, and terribly confused. One December day his hopelessness finally overcame him. He began to run through the cold forest around him, running just as he had when he was small.

"The cold winds whipped his face as he flew. The trees were lonely and bare against the sky. Finally he could run no more and he fell, exhausted, against a tree. Gasping for breath, he looked toward the heavens. And there he found an amazing sight.

"Hanging from one of the tree branches above him was a single red maple leaf. It was terribly alone, fighting dearly to hold on to its life. The winds gusted fiercely, the branches swayed violently, and the leaf was pulled in a thousand different directions. The man watched it struggle. And then, unexpectedly, the little leaf fell.

"As it fell, though, a most magical thing happened: instead of dropping lifeless upon the frost, the leaf was snatched by a rushing breeze and sent twirling through the air. Bodie smiled through his tears as he watched a dance unfold.

"Around and around the little leaf flew, skirting through the trees, rising higher and higher until it was lost in the peace of a deep and snowy sky. The man watched it all. Then he rose and returned home.

"That is my story," said the storyteller. "I am Bodie who learned about surrender from that December leaf."

Clare sat, unable to think for a moment. This was the story of the West Wind.

His father's name was Bodie.

This was his father.

For a while he didn't say anything. He just stared at the sea, watching the light play over the waves, watching the ripples form and dissolve. Then he turned to face his father. "You ran for a long time," he said.

The man slowly nodded. "Too long."

They sat by the sea, listening to the sound of the waves. The sun dipped a little lower in the sky.

Finally Clare said, "But I don't understand it. I still don't understand how you could have left us."

"It was so hard to do," said his father.

"But how?" said Clare, a bit louder this time. "How could you go?"

"At the time, I was confused," the man told him. "I needed to find my answer."

"Your *answer?*" Clare shook his head. "Is that all you care about? Your answer?"

"Yes, it is," said the man. "At the moment I surrendered—at the moment I saw the leaf drop—I finally found it."

Clare stood up and walked away from the man, toward the sea. He stared out over the waves. "And so what was it?" he said. "What did you find that was so great?"

"I found a relationship."

"A *relationship?*" asked Clare, turning around. "With who?"

"With you," said the man. "And your mother. And with everyone else I'd ever come across. That was my answer. I finally saw it."

Clare looked at his father's face and saw that his eyes were filled with tears.

He stared at the man, at the tears running down his face. He saw the confusion, the anguish, the years of struggle. And then, slowly, the image began to shift.

How did it happen? Clare never did figure it out. He simply watched the man, looked into his eyes, and allowed the scene to unfold. The years began to fall away, one by one, like heavy coats of armor. One by one they unbuckled and fell. The years of wondering, blaming, envisioning this meeting—they all fell away.

Clare simply looked, open-eyed, and he saw. He saw the answer himself. It was forgiveness and trust and a great letting go. It was a perfect love, as limitless as the sky. He saw it all in his father's eyes and he knew it was the truth.

The boy walked forward, away from the waves, into his father's arms. "Yes," he said.

"It's so simple," said his father.

And together they stood, looking out at the edge of the sea.

∾

The final trip was a sheer delight.

On the night of their reunion, Clare and his father walked back to the encampment. The man announced to the people, "Now we may go. For finally my son has arrived." A cry of joy arose from the crowd.

The group traveled for weeks on the open road, trading stories and merry laughter. Everyone was excited; the people could barely wait to reach the destination. Then, at last, they turned from the road onto a path which led straight to the gate of a garden. There they shook their heads with wonder—for it was more beautiful than the man had described. Meadows stretched away from a great wooden house; a stream bubbled in the background; birds flew into and out of a huge sweeping garden. It was truly a paradise.

The people spread out, wandering over the land. As they explored, they barely noticed a woman rising from the vegetables, coming to meet the man and his son. They barely noticed the tearful embraces, the joy, the great sense of reunion. They were too filled with wonder themselves.

And so the homecoming was a happy time. Clare and his mother and father did their best to make room for the people in the house. They unpacked the old silverware, dusted off glasses, and threw open the doors of the unused rooms. After a jubilant dinner and several toasts to friendship and the like, the family of three slipped out the back door.

They strolled through the garden as twilight fell. At last they picked a soft spot and sat down to rest. "I had dreams of a garden like this," said the man, smiling and shaking his head at the sight. "But it's even better than I imagined."

"I've had a good helper," said the woman, rustling Clare's hair.

Clare grinned. "You know, I've been thinking about it," he said. "Someday I might like to grow a garden of my own." He thought back on his journey. "You see, when I was traveling," he said, "I met some people who had gardens. Not real gardens, exactly. But the same sort of feeling."

"There's something magical about a garden," said his mother.

Clare nodded. "I mean, these people didn't have any plants around. But I felt safe when I was with them. I felt like I could grow. It was just like being in a garden."

The woman smiled. "And you'd like to create a place like that someday?"

"I think so," Clare said. He nodded. "Yeah, I think I would. Someplace where people could come together and help each other grow."

Clare's mother shifted her weight, reaching into a pocket. She pulled out a small leather bag. "Then this is for you," she said, giving the thing to her son.

"What is it?" he asked, accepting it. He opened the drawstring and poured a small pile of seeds into his hand. "Seeds?"

"They were given to us on the day you were born," the woman explained. "I've used my share. The rest are for you."

His father added, "Choose a place that needs them."

Clare looked at the seeds. He nodded and poured them back into the bag. "I will," he said.

"I saw a lot of places on my journey," said his father, "and I met a lot of people. And I know that the world is a desert without gardens like these."

The boy nodded. "I saw some deserts, too." Then he added, "But do you really think it's possible? Some places look like they're beyond help."

"Someday," said the man, "the world will be covered in gardens, down to the very last spot."

Clare smiled. "Well, then that's what I'll do," he decided. "I'll plant a garden in the sand."

His mother ran her fingers through his hair. "It'll be your gift to the world."

The little family remained in the garden until the last bit of daylight had faded around them. Clare sat quietly, looking at the plants, at the lights winking on in the house, at his mother and father. And as he sat he dreamed of starting a garden of his own.

After a while his mother and father returned to the house, and Clare stretched out upon the ground. He lay among the plants, staring at the sky, until the moon rose high above his head. In its glow he found the faces of his past.

Here was old Mr. Tannen and the red-mustached man, golden Samara and chuckling Jing. Here was Baba, dancing on the marble floors of a towering castle. Here were his mother and his father, together in a beautiful place. And here were the unseen faces of a thousand fellow travelers, marching together toward a newborn garden. Clare was glad. With a silent "thank you" offered to them all, the boy fell deep into a world of green.